THE RIDDLE OF LIFE AND DEATH

R

THE RIDDLE OF LIFE AND DEATH

—

TILLIE OLSEN AND
LEO TOLSTOY

WITH AN INTRODUCTION BY
JULES CHAMETZKY

The Feminist Press
at The City University of New York
New York

significance of falling while hanging upla vish drapes? effect of his death on the family. a good thing.

Published in 2007 by the Feminist Press at the City University of New York, The
Graduate Center, 365 Fifth Avenue, Suite 5406, New York, NY 10016

Library of Congress Cataloging-in-Publication Data

The riddle of life and death / Tillie Olsen and Leo Tolstoy ; with an introduction
by Jules Chametzky.
　　p. cm.
　ISBN-13: 978-1-55861-536-6 (pbk.)
　ISBN-10: 1-55861-536-9 (pbk.)
　I. Olsen, Tillie. Tell me a riddle. II. Tolstoy, Leo, graf, 1828-1910. Smert' Ivana
Il'icha. English. III. Title: Death of Ivan Ilych.
　PN6014.R525 2007
　813'.54—dc22

　　　　　　　　　　　　　　　　　2006030005

Text and cover design by Lisa Force
Printed in Canada

13 12 11 10 09 08 07　　　5 4 3 2 1

CONTENTS

—

INTRODUCTION

—

The grave's a fine and private place
But none, I think, do there embrace
—Andrew Marvell

. . . ask for me to-morrow and you shall find me a grave man.
—Mercutio, *Romeo and Juliet*

In an interview preceding the appearance of his recent book, *Everyman* (2006), which is about a man's life seen from the vantage point of its progress (or decline) towards the grave that begins and ends the tale, Philip Roth observes that there are many novels about adultery, but very few stories or novels—he names Thomas Mann's *The Magic Mountain*, Solzhenitsyn's *Cancer Ward*, Tolstoy's *The Death of Ivan Ilych*— about death and dying. Roth is correct, though he notably omits mentioning Tillie Olsen's *Tell Me a Riddle*, one of the great stories, along with *Ivan Ilych*, on the subject—*the* great subject, according to Henry James. Muriel Spark's *Memento Mori* also deserves mention, though its overall effect is less about the human tragedy than about its darkly comic, rueful side. Pairing Tolstoy's and Olsen's two long stories or novellas, as they are sometimes called, by the Feminist Press thus corrects an oversight while inviting sympathetic comparisons and differences between them. Both have been written about and appreciated extensively, and in at least one fine essay, compared with great insight (Banks 1995). Yet there is much to be said about each story, occasionally rehearsing previous observations, but still discovering new facets of these literary jewels.

Tolstoy's powerful story is, in essence, a *memento mori*, a poignant reminder that we all must die. He rubs that in, immediately—as Philip Roth has done, in a bold imitation of the master, by beginning his story with the death of its central character: at the site of his grave and burial.

Tolstoy begins his tale of dying and death at the funeral bier in Ivan Ilych's house. Both stories then chronicle the paths to these deaths. Roth produces a modern version of the gravedigger's scene in *Hamlet* by ending his story literally in the grave, talking with the gravedigger—and with that scene he, too, achieves a kind of humbling knowledge of life, death, dignity, and grace. Tolstoy does not need that ultimate pathos, ending his story more simply, as follows:

"It is finished!" said someone near him.
He heard these words and repeated them in his soul.
Death is finished, he said to himself. "It is no more."
He drew in a breath, stopped in the midst of a sigh,
stretched out, and died.

Death is no more—fact or pious hope? In strictest Christian belief, acceptance of Christ, who died for us all, assures eternal life—death has indeed been killed, is no more, that most ancient of hopes. Is that what Tolstoy, a believer, after all, though not in any institutional way, means his story to affirm? It is a possible reading. I prefer to cast a more humanistic light on the matter, as I think Tolstoy does, while recognizing the deeply spiritual quality that emerges at the core of Tolstoy's vision.

The feminist, radical, ethnic dimensions of Olsen's story have been fruitfully examined and documented by scholars and critics, but what has not been addressed sufficiently, it seems to me, in "Tell Me a Riddle," is its existential, agonizing, and clear-sighted address to aging, death, and dying. In Eva's suffering through to her end, there is much emotional and intellectual illumination, a kind of triumph of will, flashes of a defiant and singular soul, in addition to great, great pain that ends in terrible pathos for the survivors, as well as, in Jeannie's last words to the bereaved husband, perhaps a sign of the author's compassionate hope, a glimpse of grace. There is no doubt in my mind that Olsen also had Tolstoy somewhere in mind, though her final vision, humanistic and as full of pity and understanding of the human condition as Tolstoy's, is unambiguously more secular.

Tolstoy's story begins with a kind of social satire—comic at times in a way reminiscent of, say, Mark Twain, unlikely as that sounds. Ivan Ilych's peers and associates from his professional life, as close to friends as he has, observe the proprieties by visiting the house of mourning. They extend condolences to the widow and family, even as their first thoughts are also to calculate what Ilych's death will mean to their careers, and even though they are now impatient to get to their bridge game. Outwardly bereft, the widow is actually concerned about more practical matters. As Tolstoy observes, after the weeping and the recitation of the details of her husband's sufferings (she notes, too, how *she* had suffered, wondering how she could have borne it all), she gets down to business. Because her husband had been a civil servant of some standing, she will get a pension, about which she knows in minutest detail, Tolstoy tells us, but now she is trying to extract from Peter Ivanovich, Ilych's associate, how she can get more. When he tells her there is no way, she starts thinking of ways to be rid of him. Ivanovich remains for the service in the death-chamber, which is full of candles, groans, incense, tears, and sobs (here is where Huck Finn's commenting on a sentimental funeral scene, as being full of "tears and flapdoodle" comes to mind). He meets the preoccupied daughter and the fourteen-year-old son, whose tear-stained eyes had the look to him of boys who were not pure (self-abusers?). All of this is grim comedy, satire. Then Peter Ivanovich makes his getaway and, in the final words of the first section, he gets to his bridge game after the first rubber, when it is easy for him to cut in.

There are twelve sections in all to the story in which the tone deepens and darkens as the narrative proceeds. We are moved through satiric or implicitly critical views of the man, his family, the life he has chosen, the society in which he uncritically swims, one that fosters shallowness and conventionality, hierarchy, lack of serious self-reflection. All of that is shown: the pride in his furniture that he takes as a measure of his social success, but that is in reality just like everyone else's in his class; the pompous misdiagnoses of the doctors; the petty ego trips when he can display his powers as a magistrate. And then it all drops away at the very end. In his illness, Ilych begins to wonder how he has lived his life. He has his illumination, his moment of grace, forgiving all, and, presumably himself, for not having lived a life with meaning. It was most ordinary, he realizes, and most terrible.

At the end, what have the furniture, his house, and worldly goods, the marriage that descended into bitterness and estrangement, the vanity of petty power and self-regard meant? In his final agonies, only a peasant servant knows enough to let Ivan Ilych elevate his legs and place them on his shoulders in order to relieve his pain, a gesture of sublime fellow feeling, in which there is no master and servant, only empathy and a Lear-like compassion for all two-legged, fork'd creatures, alone in a pitiless storm. Tolstoy ends his story with his Everyman stripped bare, as we all are or will be, but he grants him relief from pain: Where is it, Ilych asks. Finally, no pain, no death, only light. And a vast pity: Ilych feels sorry for his wife, his son, for all of them (and us?), as all the accoutrements of life, all that which at the end he feels oppresses him from all sides, are stripped away. He wants to ask his family to forgive him, but the word that he manages to pronounce, in his pain, is "Forego." Forego. That could seem to argue for a religious position, but this existential awareness of the basically tragic condition we all share should also lead us, the readers of Tolstoy the master, Tolstoy the moralist, to self-examination, and an injunction to live one's life differently. Not to give allegiance to shallow values, not to be enslaved to social conventions, not to live for frivolous and ephemeral pleasures and rewards. *Du must dein leben aendern* as Rilke would later write. Think of last things, and that life is more serious than all of that.

Like Tolstoy, Olsen is a moralist, and like his, her *memento mori* is a reminder to live life better. The better in *Tell Me a Riddle*, is told from a determinedly left-feminist perspective, rooted in Olsen's tough life-long experience (b. 1912) as a woman, wife, mother, socialist, radical writer, and activist of the thirties, one of the few women writers to appear, under the maiden name of Tillie Lerner, in left and Communist publications of the time. She endured years of silence—the title of her eloquent collection of essays, *Silences* (on why women writers and putative writers have been silenced over

6

the decades of our so-called modern era), until her reemergence in the 1950s with a writing fellowship at Stanford. There she began the work here republished. Tillie Olsen came out of the working class—the "conscious working class" as was once said on the left—while Tolstoy was a Russian aristocrat living his whole life (1828–1910) within a most autocratic Czarism, fighting in its Crimean and Caucusus wars of the 1850s, writing memorably about the war against Napoleon in 1812 in one of the world's greatest novels, *War and Peace*, but in his long life drawn more and more towards a life working in his fields among the people (the peasantry in his place and time), vegetarianism, pacifism, renunciation (remember "Forego"), attempts at a Christ-like simplicity, writing tracts on peace and justice. His stature in his time is inestimable—when news of his death arrived, Maxim Gorky is said to have thrown himself upon the ground and cried, "We are all orphans now."

It would be hubristic to claim that Olsen's place in literature or in the modern feminist movement exists on that plane—for one thing, we don't live in that kind of world anymore, in which a writer could be the moral arbiter of a whole generation or even at its outermost limits, a civilization. But her stature and influence, certainly in the United States, and among women, writers, and others, especially with this work and *Silences,* cannot be overstated. And the work is about life, an Everywoman's life specifically. Olsen's work is an exhortation to feminist consciousness, and to the achievement of the full life women are entitled to. The political dimensions of the lives Olsen depicts are, of course, clear throughout.

That dignifying of the "ordinary" burdens of women's lives as they were and as they are, despite the gains feminists can record, mark all four of the stories included in the volume called *Tell Me a Riddle*. Olsen marks the heroines of the early stories, "I Stand Here Ironing," "Hey Sailor, What Ship?" and "O Yes,"—mothers, daughters, grandmothers, wives, girlfriends—with class status. They are all working their way through or suffering from, poverty or, conversely, from the separations and dislocations of family as emergent middle-class professions and educations divide and separate children and parents. Race is a powerful signifier in "O Yes," class in "Hey Sailor," and in the first story in the volume, "I Stand Here Ironing," the brilliant and defiant use of an iconic woman at an ironing board with a humble iron in hand—not the patriarchal knife of Abraham, but saying in effect as he did, "*Hineni*,"—I am here! Not in answer to a divine injunction (perhaps), ordinary but divine nonetheless. I am here. Attention must be paid.

But it is in the title story that Olsen writes of her Everywoman at the end of her life. In the first of *Tell Me a Riddle*'s four sections, Eva refuses her husband's insistence on selling their house and moving into a home. She is now determined, she says, "Never again to be forced to move to the rhythm of others." Urgently and after a long and difficult life, after poverty, after mothering a large family, she wants to be "able at last to live within, and not move to the rhythm of others." The forty-seven-year-old quarrel with her husband continues, no sentimentality for Eva or Olsen, though the bond between them exists, as we will learn. As we learn in the second part of the story about the cancer that will ultimately kill her, there, too, is a parallel with Ilych, whose unnamed, mysterious illness, beginning with a seemingly inconsequential accident, is probably a form of cancer. In the second part of Olsen's story, replete with her memories of child-rearing, Eva the grandmother rejects the behavior others expected. She will no longer dance to others' tunes. She seems remote from her grandchildren, refusing the Granny stereotype, refusing to tell them stories or a riddle. "I know no riddles," she says—but by the end we know the whole of her life is the answer to a question unasked by her family and the social world of her time. What has been the meaning of her whole life? The section ends with great poignancy and accuracy, in italics, "*Good-bye, my children.*"

The next opens with a trip to Los Angeles, "to the dwelling places of the cast-off old." And there, images of "Everywhere unused the life in them . . . everywhere unused the life . . . century after century still all in us not to grow." And there she knows she is dying.

The language rhythms, the speech patterns ("still all in us not to grow"), the cast-off old people she meets are Jewish. Eva refuses the narrowing down, however, as she sees it, of any religious or national identity. When she remembers the hospital chart asking for her race, she had answered defiantly, "Human." Okay, but the memory of her son's death in a bomber over Germany, her memories of the horrors of the twentieth century, Auschwitz, Hiroshima, played out in her mind against the incandescent revolutionary idealism of a true 1905er—that is, like those legendary souls who participated selflessly in the so-called failed Russian, non-Bolshevik revolution of 1905—are certainly part of a distinctively Jewish secular, humanistic left.

Then the great fourth part of the story, Eva's death, her thoughts, and what she says ("who in her life had spoken but seldom . . . now in dying, spoke incessantly") and the final image bequeathed to her granddaughter Jeannie. Jeannie, who was like Lisa, the noblewoman, the Tolstoyan (there we are, Olsen's debt acknowledged), who taught Eva to read and to love holy life and knowledge, and who was hanged for killing a betrayer in the Czarist prison they shared. Eva's wisdom: "life may be hated or wearied of, but never despised," and in her delirium, she says, ". . . go to Stuttgart and see where Davy [her dead flyer son] has no grave . . . and what? where millions have no graves, save air." Remember the millions who went up in chimney smoke.

Eva continues, interweaving the high, idealistic hopes of her youth with the realities of the familial struggles in poverty, the pains of those early Depression years still strong in the children; beyond that the horrors of the century. The lofty nineteenth-century sentiments from Victor Hugo and others about mankind, the banner of reason, justice, freedom, liberty, the assurance that these things shall be. And yet, of course, they have not been, at least not yet. Or only in our time and place as stirring choruses in the Broadway musical of *Les Miserables*.

This is all bitter knowledge, and coupled with the pain, the writhing body, the vomit, the unused life that should have been, could lead one to despair or cynicism. Yet the genius of the story and its ending is that the larger tragedy of a single death—the fifth act of every life—as told by Olsen, can also be read as an injunction to seek to live that fuller life. Furthermore, that even within the hardships and the quarrels of Grandaddy and Grandma throughout their lives, there was also joy. Despite the forty-seven-year-long struggle, he feels for her, the poor soul, the poor woman—and in *her* need she reaches out to grasp his hand, which is there to be "enfolded."

Holding the image of their clasped hands, sketched by Jeannie, Eva's husband, "as if he had been instructed . . . went back to his bed, holding the sketch (as if it could shield against the monstrous shapes of loss, of betrayal, of death) and with his free hand took hers back into his." That is how Jeannie finds them the next morning, the last day of Eva's life, a day of perpetual agony. When the man cannot bear it and leaves the room, Jeannie follows him, urging him to come back. Jeannie tells him that Granny had promised her that on her last day she would go where she first heard music, where there was a wedding in progress with dancing and joyous flutes sounding in the air: "Leave her there, Grandaddy, it is all right. She promised me. Come back. Come back and help her poor body to die."

One cannot say enough about the ending. Throughout the story, the prose is mainly direct speech capturing the voices especially of Eva and her husband. At the end, without ornament, the language surges with feeling and grace, even more powerfully. Are we being given only a rhetorical flourish, or like Ivan Ilych's ending a purifying vision of last things, in which the poor body dies, as Jeannie invites us to come and witness, wishing us to see, too, that it is "only" the frail human body, after all? Hard as it is to face or believe in this reality, in which one's heart can break at the loss, Olsen suggests that spirit, hope, and strength can, indeed, be passed on to a new generation.

> Jules Chametzky
> Professor, *emeritus*
> University of Massachusetts/Amherst

WORKS CITED

Banks, Joanne Trautmann. 1995. "Death Labors." In *"Tell Me a Riddle": Tillie Olsen.* Edited and with an Introduction by Deborah Silverton Rosenfelt. New Brunswick, N.J.: Rutgers University Press, 199–211.

LEO TOLSTOY

THE DEATH OF IVAN ILYCH

■

I

During an interval in the Melvinsky trial in the large build-
ing of the Law Courts the members and public prosecutor
met in Ivan Egorovich Shebek's private room, where the
conversation turned to the celebrated Krasovsky case. Fedor
Vasilievich fervently declared that it was not subject to their
jurisdiction, Ivan Egorovich maintained the contrary, while
Peter Ivanovich, not having entered into the discussion at
the start, took no part in it, but looked through the *Gazette*
which he had just been handed.

"Gentlemen," he said, "Ivan Ilych has died!"

"You don't say so!"

"Here, read it yourself," replied Peter Ivanovich, hand-
ing Fedor Vasilievich the paper still damp from the press.
Surrounded by a black border were the words: "Praskovya
Fedorovna Golovina, with profound sorrow, informs rela-
tives and friends of the demise of her beloved husband Ivan
Ilych Golovin, Member of the Court of Justice, which

occurred on February the 4th of this year 1882. The funeral will take place on Friday at one o'clock in the afternoon."

Ivan Ilych had been a colleague of the gentlemen present and was liked by them all. He had been ill for some weeks with an illness said to be incurable. His post had been kept open for him, but there had been conjectures that in case of his death Alexeev might receive his appointment, and that either Vinnikov or Shtabel would succeed Alexeev. So on receiving the news of Ivan Ilych's death the first thought of each of the gentlemen present in that private room was about the changes and promotions it might occasion among themselves or their acquaintances.

"I shall be sure to get Shtabel's place or Vinnikov's," thought Fedor Vasilievich. "I was promised that long ago, and the promotion means an extra eight hundred rubles a year for me besides the allowance."

"Now I must apply for my brother-in-law's transfer from Kaluga," thought Peter Ivanovich. "My wife will be very pleased, and then she won't be able to say that I never do anything for her relatives."

"I thought he would never leave his bed again," said Peter Ivanovich aloud. "It's very sad."

"But what was really the matter with him?"

"The doctors couldn't say—at least they could, but each of them said something different. When last I saw him I though he was getting better."

"I haven't been to see him since the holidays. I always meant to go."

"Did he have any property?"

"I think his wife had a little—but something quiet unimportant."

"We shall have to go to see her, but they live so terribly far away."

"Far from you, you mean. Everything's far away from your place."

"You see, he never can forgive my living on the other side of the river," said Peter Ivanovich, smiling at Shebek. Then, still talking of the distances between different parts of the city, they returned to the Court.

Besides considerations as to the possible transfers and promotions likely to result from Ivan Ilych's death, the mere fact of the death of a near acquaintance aroused, as usual, in all who heard of it the complacent feeling that, "it's he who is dead and not I."

Each one thought or felt, "Well, he's dead but I'm alive!" But the more intimate of Ivan Ilych's acquaintances, his so-called friends, could not help also thinking that now they would have to fulfil the very tiresome demands of propriety by attending the funeral service and paying a condolence call on the widow.

Fedor Vasilievich and Peter Ivanovich had been his nearest acquaintances. Peter Ivanovich had studied law with Ivan Ilych and had considered himself to be under obligations to him.

Having told his wife at dinner of Ivan Ilych's death, and of his conjecture that it might be possible to get her brother transferred to their circuit, Peter Ivanovich sacrificed his usual nap, put on his evening clothes and drove to Ivan Ilych's house.

At the entrance stood a carriage and two cabs. Leaning against the wall in the hall downstairs near the coat-stand was a coffin-lid covered with cloth of gold, ornamented with gold cord and tassels, that had been polished with metal powder. Two ladies in black were taking off their fur cloaks. Peter Ivanovich recognized one of them as Ivan Ilych's sister, but the other was a stranger to him. His colleague Schwartz was just coming downstairs, but on seeing Peter Ivanovich enter he stopped and winked at him, as if to say: "Ivan Ilych has made a mess of things—not like you and me."

Schwartz's face with his Piccadilly whiskers, and his slim figure in evening dress, as usual had an air of elegant solemnity which contrasted with the playfulness of his character and had a special piquancy here, or so it seemed to Peter Ivanovich.

Peter Ivanovich allowed the ladies to precede him and slowly followed them upstairs. Schwartz did not come down but remained where he was, and Peter Ivanovich understood that he wanted to arrange where they should play bridge that evening. The ladies went upstairs to the widow's room, and Schwartz with seriously compressed lips but a playful look in his eyes, indicated by a twist of his eyebrows the room to the right where the body lay.

Peter Ivanovich, like everyone else on such occasions, entered feeling uncertain what he would have to do. All he knew was that at such times it is always safe to cross oneself.

But he was not quite sure whether one should bow while doing so. He therefore adopted a middle course. On entering the room he began crossing himself and made a slight movement resembling a bow. At the same time, as far as the motion of his head and arm allowed, he surveyed the room. Two young men—apparently nephews, one of whom was a high-school pupil—were leaving the room, crossing themselves as they did so. An old woman was standing motionless, and a lady with strangely arched eyebrows was saying something to her in a whisper. A vigorous, resolute Church Reader, in a frock-coat, was reading something in a loud voice with an expression that precluded any contradiction. The butler's assistant, Gerasim, stepping lightly in front of Peter Ivanovich, was strewing something on the floor. Noticing this, Peter Ivanovich was immediately aware of a faint odor of a decomposing body.

The last time he had called on Ivan Ilych, Peter Ivanovich had seen Gerasim in the study. Ivan Ilych had been particularly fond of him and he was performing the duty of a sick nurse.

Peter Ivanovich continued to make the sign of the cross slightly inclining his head in an intermediate direction between the coffin, the Reader, and the icons on the table in a corner of the room. Afterwards, when it seemed to him that this movement of his arm in crossing himself had gone on too long, he stopped and began to look at the corpse.

The dead man lay, as dead men always lie, in a specially heavy way, his rigid limbs sunk in the soft cushions of the coffin, with the head forever bowed on the pillow. His yellow waxen brow with bald patches over his sunken temples was thrust up in the way peculiar to the dead, the protruding nose seeming to press on the upper lip. He was much changed and had grown even thinner since Peter Ivanovich had last seen him, but, as is always the case with the dead, his face was handsomer and above all more dignified than when he was alive. The expression on the face said that what was necessary had been accomplished, and accomplished rightly. Besides this there was in that expression a reproach and a warning to the living. This warning seemed out of place to Peter Ivanovich, or at least not applicable to him. He felt a certain discomfort and so he hurriedly crossed himself once more, turned and went out the door—too hurriedly and regardless of propriety, as he himself was aware.

Schwartz was waiting for him in the adjoining room with legs spread wide apart and both hands toying with his top-hat behind his back. The mere sight of that playful, well-groomed, and elegant figure restored Peter Ivanovich. He felt that Schwartz stood above all these happenings and would not surrender to any depressing influences. His very look said that this incident of a church service for Ivan Ilych could not be a sufficient reason for infringing the order of the session—in other words, that it would certainly not prevent his unwrapping a new pack of cards and shuffling them that evening while a footman placed four fresh candles on the table: in fact, that there was no reason for supposing that this incident would hinder their spending the evening agreeably. Indeed he said this in a whisper as Peter Ivanovich passed him, proposing that they should meet for a game at Fedor Vasilievich's. But apparently Peter Ivanovich was not destined to play bridge that evening. Praskovya Fedorovna (a short, fat woman who despite all efforts to the contrary had continued to broaden steadily from her shoulders downwards and who had the same extraordinarily arched eyebrows as the lady who had been standing by the coffin), dressed all in black, her head covered with lace, came out of her own room with some other ladies, conducted them to the room where the dead body lay, and said: "The service will begin immediately. Please go in."

Schwartz, making an indefinite bow, stood still, evidently neither accepting nor declining this invitation. Praskovya Fedorovna recognizing Peter Ivanovich, sighed, went up close to him, took his hand, and said: "I know you were a true friend to Ivan Ilych . . ." and looked at him awaiting some suitable response. And Peter Ivanovich knew that, just as it had been the right thing to cross himself in that room, what he had to do here was press her hand, sigh, and say, "Believe me . . ." So he did all this and as he did it felt that the desired result had been achieved: both he and she were touched.

"Come with me. I want to speak to you before it begins," said the widow. "Give me your arm."

Peter Ivanovich gave her his arm and they went to the inner rooms, passing Schwartz who winked at Peter Ivanovich compassionately.

"That does it for our bridge! Don't object if we find

another player. Perhaps you can cut in when you do escape," said his playful look.

Peter Ivanovich sighed still more deeply and despondently, and Praskovya Fedorovna pressed his arm gratefully. When they reached the drawing-room, upholstered in pink cretonne and lighted by a dim lamp, they sat down at the table—she on a sofa and Peter Ivanovich on a low pouffe, the springs of which yielded spasmodically under his weight. Praskovya Fedorovna had been on the point of warning him to take another seat, but felt that such a warning was out of keeping with her present condition and so she changed her mind. As he sat down on the pouffe Peter Ivanovich recalled how Ivan Ilych had arranged this room and had consulted him regarding this pink cretonne with green leaves. The whole room was full of furniture and knick-knacks, and on her way to the sofa the lace of the widow's black shawl caught on the carved edge of the table. Peter Ivanovich rose to detach it, and the springs of the pouffe, relieved of his weight, rose also and gave him a push. The widow began detaching her shawl herself, and Peter Ivanovich again sat down, suppressing the rebellious springs of the pouffe under him. But the widow had not quite freed herself and Peter Ivanovich got up again, and again the pouffe rebelled and even creaked. When this was all over she took out a clean cambric handkerchief and began to weep. The episode with the shawl and the struggle with the pouffe had cooled Peter Ivanovich's emotions and he sat there with a sullen look on his face. This awkward situation was interrupted by Sokolov, Ivan Ilych's butler, who came to report that the plot in the cemetery that Praskovya Fedorovna had chosen would cost two hundred rubles. She stopped weeping and, looking at Peter Ivanovich with the air of a victim, remarked in French that it was very hard for her. Peter Ivanovich made a silent gesture signifying his full conviction that it must indeed be so.

"You may smoke," she said in a magnanimous yet crushed voice, and turned to discuss the price of the plot for the grave with Sokolov.

While lighting his cigarette Peter Ivanovich heard her inquiring very circumstantially into the prices of different plots in the cemetery and finally decide which one she would take. When that was done she gave instructions about engaging the choir. Sokolov then left the room.

"I look after everything myself," she told Peter Ivanovich, shifting the albums that lay on the table; and noticing that the table was endangered by his cigarette-ash, she immediately passed him an ash-tray, saying as she did so: "I consider it an affectation to say that my grief prevents me attending to practical affairs. On the contrary, if anything can—I won't say console me, but—distract me, it is seeing to everything concerning him." Once again she took out her handkerchief as if preparing to cry, but suddenly, as if mastering her feeling, she shook herself and began to speak calmly. "But there is something I want to talk to you about."

Peter Ivanovich bowed, keeping control of the springs of the pouffe, which immediately began quivering under him.

"He suffered terribly during the last few days."

"Did he?" said Peter Ivanovich.

"Oh, terribly! He screamed unceasingly, not for minutes but for hours. For the last three days he screamed incessantly. It was unendurable. I cannot understand how I stood it; you could hear him three rooms away. Oh, what I have suffered!"

"Is it possible that he was conscious all that time?" asked Peter Ivanovich.

"Yes," she whispered. "To the last moment. He took leave of us a quarter of an hour before he died, and asked us to take Volodya away."

The thought of the suffering of this man whom he had known so intimately, first as a cheerful little boy, then as a schoolmate, and later as a grown-up colleague, suddenly struck Peter Ivanovich with horror, despite an unpleasant consciousness of his own and this woman's dissimulation. He saw that brow again, and that nose pressing down on the lip, and he felt afraid for himself.

"Three days of frightful suffering and then the death! Why, that might suddenly, at any time, happen to me," he thought, and for a moment felt terrified. But—he did not know how—the customary reflection at once occurred to him that this terrible thing had happened to Ivan Ilych and not to him, and that it should not and could not happen to him, and that to think that it could would be yielding to depression which he ought not to do, as Schwartz's expression plainly showed. After this reflection Peter Ivanovich felt reassured, and began to ask with interest about the details of

Ivan Ilych's death, as though death was an accident natural to Ivan Ilych but certainly not to himself.

After many details of the really dreadful physical sufferings Ivan Ilych had endured (which details he learned only from the effect those sufferings had produced on Praskovya Fedorovna's nerves) the widow apparently found it necessary to get down to business.

"Oh, Peter Ivanovich, how hard it is! How terribly, terribly hard!" and she began to weep again.

Peter Ivanovich sighed and waited for her to finish blowing her nose. When she had done so he said, "Believe me . . ." and again she began talking and brought out what was evidently her chief concern with him—namely, to question him as to how she could obtain a grant of money from the government on the occasion of her husband's death. She made it appear that she was asking Peter Ivanovich's advice about her pension, but he soon saw that she already knew about that to the minutest detail, more even than he did himself. She knew how much could be procured from the government in consequence of her husband's death, but wanted to find out whether she could possibly extract some more. Peter Ivanovich tried to think of some means of doing so, but after reflecting for a while and, out of propriety, condemning the government for its niggardliness, said he thought that nothing more could be got. Then she sighed and evidently began to devise some means of getting rid of her visitor. Noticing this, he put out his cigarette, rose, pressed her hand, and went out into the anteroom.

In the dining-room where the clock stood that Ivan Ilych had liked so much and had bought at an antique shop, Peter Ivanovich met a priest and a few acquaintances who had come to attend the service, and he recognized Ivan Ilych's daughter, a handsome young woman. She was dressed in black and her slim figure appeared slimmer than ever. She had a gloomy, determined, almost angry expression, and bowed to Peter Ivanovich as though he were in some way to blame. Behind her, with the same offended look, stood a wealthy young man, an examining magistrate, whom Peter Ivanovich also knew and who was her fiancé, as he had heard. He bowed mournfully to them and was about to pass into the death-chamber, when from under the stairs appeared the figure of Ivan Ilych's schoolboy son, who looked extremely like his father. He seemed a little Ivan Ilych, such as Peter Ivanovich remembered when they studied law together. His tear-stained eyes had in them the look that is seen in the eyes of boys of thirteen or fourteen who are not pure-minded. When he saw Peter Ivanovich he scowled morosely and shamefacedly. Peter Ivanovich nodded to him and entered the death-chamber. The service began: candles, groans, incense, tears, and sobs. Peter Ivanovich stood looking gloomily down at his feet. He did not look at the dead man once, did not yield to any depressing influence, and was one of the first to leave the room. There was no one in the anteroom, but Gerasim darted out of the dead man's room, rummaged with his strong hands among the fur coats to find Peter Ivanovich's, and helped him on with it.

"Well, friend Gerasim," said Peter Ivanovich, so as to say something. "It's a sad affair, isn't it?"

"It's God will. We shall all come to it some day," said Gerasim, displaying his teeth—the even, white teeth of a healthy peasant—and, like a man in the thick of urgent work, he briskly opened the front door, called the coachman, helped Peter Ivanovich into the sledge, and sprang back to the porch as if in readiness for what he had to do next.

Peter Ivanovich found the fresh air particularly pleasant after the smell of incense, the dead body, and carbolic acid.

"Where to, sir?" asked the coachman.

"It's still not too late. . . . I'll call on Fedor Vasilievich."

Accordingly he drove there and found them just finishing the first rubber, so that it was quite convenient for him to cut in.

II

Ivan Ilych's life had been most simple and most ordinary and therefore most terrible.

He had been a member of the Court of Justice, and died at the age of forty-five. His father had been an official who after serving in various ministries and departments in Petersburg had made the sort of career which brings men to positions from which by reason of their long service they cannot be dismissed, though they are obviously unfit to hold any responsible position, and for whom therefore posts are specially created, which though fictitious carry salaries of from six to ten thousand rubles that are not fictitious, in receipt of which they live on to a great age.

Such was the Privy Councillor and superfluous member of various superfluous institutions, Ilya Epimovich Golovin.

He had three sons, of whom Ivan Ilych was the second. The eldest son was following in his father's footsteps only in another department, and was already approaching that stage in the service at which a similar sinecure would be reached. The third son was a failure. He had ruined his prospects in a number of positions and was now serving in the railway department. His father and brothers, and still more their wives, not merely disliked meeting him, but avoided re-membering his existence unless compelled to do so. His sister had married Baron Greff, a Petersburg official of her father's type. Ivan Ilych was *le phénix de la famille*[1] as people said. He was neither as cold and formal as his elder brother nor as wild as the younger; he was a happy mean between them—an intelligent, polished, lively and agreeable man. He had studied with his younger brother at the School of Law, but the latter had failed to complete the course and was expelled when he was in his fifth year. Ivan Ilych finished the course well. Even when he was at the School of Law he was just what he remained for the rest of his life: a capable, cheerful, good-natured, and sociable man, though strict in the fulfilment of what he considered to be his duty. And he considered his duty to be what was so considered by those in authority. Neither as a boy nor as a man was he a toady, but from early youth he was by nature attracted to people of high station as a fly is drawn to the light, assimilating their ways and views of life and establishing friendly relations with them. All the enthusiasms of childhood and youth passed without leaving much trace on him; he succumbed to sensuality, to vanity, and recently among the highest classes to liberalism, but always within limits which his instinct unfailingly indicated to him as correct.

At school he had done things which had formerly seemed to him very horrid and made him feel disgusted with himself when he did them; but later on when he saw that such actions were done by people of good position and that they did not regard them as wrong, he was not exactly able to regard them as right, but to forget about them entirely or not be troubled at all by remembering them.

Having graduated from the School of Law and qualified for the tenth rank of the civil service, and having received money from his father for his equipment, Ivan Ilych ordered himself clothes at Scharmer's, the fashionable tailor, hung a medallion inscribed *respice finem*[2] on his watch-chain, took leave of his professor and the prince who was patron of the school, had a farewell dinner with his comrades at Donon's first-class restaurant, and with his new and fashionable portmanteau, linen, clothes, shaving and other toilet articles, and a traveling rug, all purchased at the best shops, he set off for one of the provinces where, through his father's influence, he had been attached to the governor as an official for special service.

In the province Ivan Ilych soon arranged as easy and

agreeable a position for himself as he enjoyed at the School of Law. He performed his official task, established his career, and at the same time amused himself pleasantly and decorously. Occasionally he paid official visits to country districts where he behaved with dignity both to his superiors and inferiors, and performed the duties entrusted to him, which related chiefly to the schismatics,[3] with an exactness and incorruptible honesty of which he could not but feel proud.

In official matters, despite his youth and taste for frivolous gaiety, he was exceedingly reserved, punctilious, and even severe; but in society he was often amusing and witty, always good-natured, correct in his manner, and *bon enfant*,[4] as the governor and his wife—with whom he was like one of the family—used to say of him.

In the province he had an affair with a lady who made advances to the elegant young lawyer, and there was also a milliner; and there were carousals with aides-de-camp who visited the district, and after-supper visits to a certain outlying street of doubtful reputation; and there was also some obsequiousness to his chief and even to his chief's wife, but all this was done with such a tone of good breeding that no harsh names could be applied to it. It all came under the heading of the French saying: "*Il faut que jeunesse se passe*."[5] It was all done with clean hands, in clean linen, with French phrases, and above all among people of the best society and consequently with the approval of people of rank.

So Ivan Ilych served for five years and then came a change in his official life. The new and reformed judicial institutions were introduced, and new men were needed. Ivan Ilych became such a new man. He was offered the post of examining magistrate, and he accepted it though the post was in another province and required him to give up the connections he had formed and to make new ones. His friends met to give him a send-off; they had a group-photograph taken and presented him with a silver cigarette-case, and he set off to his new post.

As examining magistrate Ivan Ilych was just as *comme il faut*[6] and decorous a man, inspiring general respect and capable of separating his official duties from his private life, as he had been when acting as an official on special service. His duties now as examining magistrate were far more interesting and attractive than before. In his former position it had been pleasant to wear an everyday uniform made by Scharmer, and to pass through the crowd of petitioners and officials who were timorously awaiting an audience with the governor, and who envied him as with a free and easy gait he went straight into his chief's private room to have a cup of tea and a cigarette with him. But not many people had then been directly dependent on him—only police officials and the sectarians when he went on special missions—and he liked to treat them politely, almost as comrades, as if he were letting them feel that he who had the power to crush them was treating them in this simple, friendly way. Then there were only a few such people. But now, as an examining magistrate, Ivan Ilych felt that everyone without exception, even the most important and self-satisfied, was in his power, and that he need only write a few words on a sheet of paper with a certain heading, and this or that important, self-satisfied person would be brought before him in the role of an accused party or a witness, and if he did not choose to allow him to sit down, would have to stand before him and answer his questions. Ivan Ilych never abused his power; on the contrary he tried to soften its expression, but the consciousness of it and the possibility of softening its effect, supplied the chief interest and attraction of his office. In his work itself, especially in his examinations, he very soon acquired a method of eliminating all considerations irrelevant to the legal aspect of the case, and reducing even the most complicated case to a form in which it would be presented on paper only in its externals, completely excluding his personal opinion of the matter, while above all observing every prescribed formality. The work was new and Ivan Ilych was one of the first men to apply the new Code of 1864.[7]

On taking up the post of examining magistrate in a new town, he made new acquaintances and connections, placed himself on a new footing, and assumed a somewhat different tone. He took up an attitude of rather dignified aloofness towards the provincial authorities, but picked out the best circle of legal gentlemen and wealthy gentry living in town and assumed a tone of slight dissatisfaction with the government, of moderate liberalism, and of enlightened citizenship. At the same time, without at all altering the elegance of his toilet, he ceased shaving his chin and allowed his beard to grow as it pleased.

Ivan Ilych settled down very pleasantly in this new town. The society there, which inclined towards opposition to the governor, was friendly, his salary was larger, and he began to play *vint*,[8] which he found added considerably to the pleasure of life, for he had a capacity for cards, played good-humoredly, and calculated rapidly and astutely, so that he usually won.

After living there for two years he met his future wife, Praskovya Fedorovna Mikhel, who was the most attractive, clever, and brilliant girl of the set in which he moved, and among other amusements and relaxations from his labors as examining magistrate, Ivan Ilych established light and playful relations with her.

While he had been an official on special service he had been accustomed to dance, but, as an examining magistrate it was exceptional for him to do so. If he danced now, he did it as if to show that though he served under the reformed order of things, and had reached the fifth official rank, still when it came to dancing he could do it better than most people. So at the end of an evening he sometimes danced with Praskovya Fedorovna, and it was chiefly during these dances that he captivated her. She fell in love with him. At first Ivan Ilych had no definite intention of marrying, but when the girl fell in love with him he said to himself: "Really, why shouldn't I marry?"

Praskovya Fedorovna came of a good family, was not bad looking, and had a bit of property. Ivan Ilych might have aspired to a more brilliant match, but even this was good. He had his salary, and she, he hoped, would have an equal income. She was well connected, and was a sweet, pretty, thoroughly correct young woman. To say that Ivan Ilych married because he fell in love with Praskovya Fedorovna and found that she sympathized with his views of life would be as incorrect as to say that he married because his social circle approved of the match. He was swayed by both these considerations: the marriage gave him personal satisfaction, and at the same time it was considered the right thing to do by the most highly placed of his associates.

So Ivan Ilych got married.

The preparations for marriage and the beginning of married life, with its conjugal caresses, new furniture, new crockery, and new linen, were very pleasant until his wife became pregnant—so that Ivan Ilych had begun to think that marriage would not impair the easy, agreeable, pleasant and always decorous character of his life, approved of by society and regarded by himself as natural, but would even improve it. But from the first months of his wife's pregnancy, something new, unpleasant, depressing, and unseemly, from which there was no way of escape, unexpectedly showed itself.

His wife, without any reason—*de gaieté de cœur*[9] as Ivan Ilych expressed it to himself—began to disturb the pleasure and propriety of their life. She began to be jealous without cause, expected him to devote his whole attention to her; she found fault with everything, and made coarse and illmannered scenes.

At first Ivan Ilych hoped to escape from the unpleasant-

36

ness of this state of affairs by the same easy and decorous relation to life that had served him heretofore: he tried to ignore his wife's disagreeable moods, continued to live in his usual easy and pleasant way, invited friends to his house for a game of cards, and also tried going out to his club or spending his evenings with friends. But one day his wife began upbraiding him so vigorously, using such coarse words, and continued to abuse him every time he did not fulfil her demands, so resolutely and with such evident determination not to give way till he submitted—that is, till he stayed at home and was bored just as she was—that he became alarmed. He now realized that matrimony—at any rate with Praskovya Fedorovna—was not always conducive to the pleasures and amenities of life, but on the contrary often infringed both comfort and propriety, and that he must therefore entrench himself against such infringement. And Ivan Ilych began to seek means of doing so. His official duties were the one thing that imposed upon Praskovya Fedorovna, and by means of his official work and the duties attached to it he began struggling with his wife to secure his own independence.

With the birth of their child, attempts to feed it and the various failures in doing so, and with the real and imaginary illnesses of mother and child, in which Ivan Ilych's sympathy was demanded but about which he understood nothing, the need of securing for himself an existence outside his family life became still more imperative.

As his wife grew more irritable and exacting and Ivan Ilych transferred the center of gravity of his life more and more to his official work, so did he grow to like his work better and became more ambitious than before.

Very soon, within a year of his wedding, Ivan Ilych had realized that marriage, though it may add some comforts to life, is in fact a very intricate and difficult affair towards which in order to perform one's duty, that is, to lead a decorous life approved of by society, one must adopt a definite attitude, just as towards one's official duties.

And Ivan Ilych evolved such an attitude towards married life. He only required of it those conveniences—dinner at home, housewife, and bed—which it could give him, and above all that propriety of external forms required by public opinion. For the rest he looked for light-hearted pleasure and propriety, and was very thankful when he found them, but if he met with antagonism and querulousness he retired at once into his separate fenced-off world of official duties, where he found satisfaction.

Ivan Ilych was esteemed a good official, and after three years was made Assistant Public Prosecutor. His new duties, their importance, the possibility of indicting and imprisoning anyone he chose, the publicity his speeches received, and the success he had in all these things, made his work still more attractive.

More children came. His wife became more and more querulous and ill-tempered, but the attitude Ivan Ilych had adopted towards his home life rendered him almost impervious to her grumbling.

After seven years' service in that town he was transferred

to another province as Public Prosecutor. They moved, but were short of money and his wife did not like the place they moved to. Though the salary was higher the cost of living was greater, besides which two of their children died and family life became still more unpleasant for him.

Praskovya Fedorovna blamed her husband for every inconvenience they encountered in their new home. Most of the conversations between husband and wife, especially as to the children's education, led to topics which recalled former disputes, and these disputes were apt to flare up again at any moment. There remained only those rare periods of amorousness which still came to them at times but did not last long. These were islets at which they anchored for a while and then again set out upon that ocean of veiled hostility which showed itself in their aloofness from one another. This aloofness might have grieved Ivan Ilych had he considered that it ought not to exist, but now he regarded the position as normal, and even made it the goal at which he aimed in family life. His aim was to free himself more and more from those unpleasantnesses and to give them a semblance of harmlessness and propriety. He attained this by spending less and less time with his family, and when obliged to be at home he tried to safeguard his position by the presence of outsiders. The chief thing however was that he had his official duties. The whole interest of his life now centered in the official world and that interest absorbed him. The consciousness of his power, being able to ruin anybody he wished to ruin, the importance, even the external dignity of his entry into court, or meetings with his subordinates, his success with superiors and inferiors, and above all his masterly handling of cases, of which he was conscious—all this gave him pleasure and filled his life, together with chats with his colleagues, dinners, and bridge. So that on the whole Ivan Ilych's life continued to flow as he considered it should do—pleasantly and properly.

So things continued for another seven years. His eldest daughter was already sixteen, another child had died, and only one son was left, a schoolboy and a subject of dissension. Ivan Ilych wanted to put him in the School of Law, but to spite him Praskovya Fedorovna entered him at the High School. The daughter had been educated at home and had turned out well: the boy did not learn badly either.

III

So Ivan Ilych lived for seventeen years after his marriage. He was already a Public Prosecutor of long standing, and had declined several proposed transfers while awaiting a more desirable post, when an unanticipated and unpleasant occurrence quite upset the peaceful course of his life. He was expecting to be offered the post of presiding judge in a University town, but Happe somehow came to the front and obtained the appointment instead. Ivan Ilych became irritable, reproached Happe, and quarrelled both him and with his immediate superiors—who became colder to him and again passed him over when other appointments were made.

This was in 1880, the hardest year of Ivan Ilych's life. It

was then that it became evident on the one hand that his salary was insufficient for them to live on, and on the other that he had been forgotten, and not only that; what was for him the greatest and most cruel injustice appeared to others as quite an ordinary occurrence. Even his father did not consider it his duty to help him. Ivan Ilych felt himself abandoned by everyone; they regarded his position with a salary of three thousand five hundred rubles as quite normal and even fortunate. He alone knew that with the consciousness of the injustices done him, with his wife's incessant nagging, and with the debts he had contracted by living beyond his means, his position was far from normal.

In order to save money that summer he obtained a leave of absence and went away with his wife to live in the country at her brother's place.

There, without his work, he experienced boredom for the first time in his life, and not only boredom but intolerable depression. He decided it was impossible to go on living this way, and that it was necessary to take energetic measures.

Having passed a sleepless night pacing up and down the veranda, he decided to go to Petersburg and bestir himself, in order to punish those who had failed to appreciate him and to get transferred to another ministry.

Next day, despite many protests from his wife and her brother, he started for Petersburg with the sole object of obtaining a post with a salary of five thousand rubles a year. He was no longer bent on any particular department, or tendency, or kind of activity. Now all he wanted was an appointment to another post with a salary of five thousand rubles, either in the administration, in the banks, with the railways in one of the Empress Marya's Institutions,[10] or even in the customs—but it had provide a salary of five thousand rubles and be in a ministry other than the one in which they had failed to appreciate him.

And this quest of Ivan Ilych's was crowned with remarkable and unexpected success. At Kursk an acquaintance of his, F.I. Ilyin, got into the first-class carriage, sat down beside Ivan Ilych, and told him about a telegram just received by the governor of Kursk announcing that a change was about to take place in the ministry: Peter Ivanovich was to be superseded by Ivan Semenovich.

The proposed change, apart from its significance for Russia, had a special significance for Ivan Ilych, because by bringing forward a new man, Peter Petrovich, and consequently his friend Zakhar Ivanovich, it was highly favorable for Ivan Ilych, since Zakhar Ivanovich was a friend and colleague of his.

In Moscow this news was confirmed, and on reaching Petersburg Ivan Ilych found Zakhar Ivanovich and received a definite promise of an appointment in his former Department of Justice.

A week later he telegraphed his wife: "Zakhar in Miller's place. I shall receive appointment on presentation of report."

Thanks to this change of personnel, Ivan Ilych had unexpectedly obtained an appointment in his former ministry which placed him two stages above his former colleagues besides giving him five thousand rubles salary and three thousand five hundred rubles for expenses connected with his transfer. All his ill humor towards his former enemies and the whole department vanished, and Ivan Ilych was completely happy.

He returned to the country more cheerful and contented than he had been for a long time. Praskovya Fedorovna also cheered up and a truce was arranged between them. Ivan Ilych told of how he had been fêted by everybody in Petersburg, how all those who had been his enemies were put to shame and now fawned on him, how envious they were of his appointment, and how much everybody in Petersburg had liked him.

Praskovya Fedorovna listened to all this and appeared to believe it. She did not contradict anything, but only made plans for their life in the town to which they were going. Ivan Ilych saw with delight that these plans were his plans, that he and his wife agreed, and that, after a stumble, his life was regaining its due and natural character of pleasant lightheartedness and decorum.

Ivan Ilych had come back for a short time only, for he had to take up his new duties on the 10th of September. Moreover, he needed time to settle into the new place, to move all his belongings from the province, and to buy and order many additional things: in a word, to make arrangements as he had resolved on, which were almost exactly what Praskovya Fedorovna had also decided on.

Now that everything had happened so fortunately, and he and his wife were at one in their aims and moreover saw so little of one another, they got on together better than they had done since the first years of their marriage. Ivan Ilych had thought of taking his family away with him at once, but the insistence of his wife's brother and her sister-in-law, who had suddenly become particularly amiable and friendly to him and his family, induced him to depart alone.

So he left, and the cheerful state of mind induced by his success and by the harmony between his wife and himself, the one intensifying the other, did not desert him. He found a delightful house, just the thing both he and his wife had dreamt about. Spacious, lofty reception rooms in the old style, a convenient and dignified study, rooms for his wife and daughter, a study for his son—it might have been made to order for them. Ivan Ilych himself oversaw all the arrangements, chose the wallpapers, supplemented the furniture (preferably with antiques which he considered particularly *comme il faut*), and supervised the upholstering. Everything progressed and approached the ideal he had set himself: even when things were only half completed they exceeded his expectations. He saw what a refined and elegant character, free from vulgarity, it would all have when it was ready. On falling asleep he pictured to himself how the reception-room would look. Looking at the yet unfinished drawing-room he could see the fireplace, the screen, the bookcase, the little chairs dotted here and there, the dishes and plates on the walls, and the bronzes, as they would be when everything was in place. He was pleased by the thought of how his wife and daughter, who shared his taste in this matter, would be impressed by it. They were certainly not expecting as much. He had been particularly successful in finding, and buying cheaply, antiques which gave a particularly aristocratic character to the whole place. But in his letters he intentionally understated everything in order to be able to surprise them. All this so absorbed him that his new duties—though he liked his official work—interested him less than he had expected. Sometimes he even had moments of absent-mindedness during the court sessions and would consider whether he should have straight or curved cornices for his curtains. He was so interested in it all that he often did things himself, rearranging the furniture, or rehanging the curtains. Once when mounting a step-ladder to show the upholsterer, who did not understand, how he wanted the hangings draped, he mad a false step and slipped, but being a strong and agile man he clung on and only knocked his side against the knob of the window frame. The bruised place was painful but the pain soon passed, and he felt particularly bright and well just then. He wrote: "I feel fifteen years younger." He thought he would have everything ready by September, but it dragged on till mid-October. The result was charming not only in his eyes but to everyone who saw it.

In reality it was just what is usually seen in the houses of people of moderate means who want to appear rich, and therefore succeed only in resembling others like themselves: there are damasks, dark wood, plants, rugs, and dull and polished bronzes—all the things people of a certain class have in order to resemble other people of that class. His house was so like the others that it would never have been noticed, but to him it all seemed to be quite exceptional. He was very happy when he met his family at the station and brought them to the newly furnished house all lit up, where a footman in a white tie opened the door into the hall decorated with plants, and when they went on into the drawing-room and the study uttering exclamations of delight. He conducted them everywhere, drank in their praises eagerly, and beamed with delight. At tea that evening, when Praskovya Fedorovna among others things asked him about his fall, he laughed, and showed them how he had gone flying and had frightened the upholsterer.

"It's a good thing I'm a bit of an athlete. Another man might have been killed, but I merely knocked myself, just here; it hurts when it's touched, but it's passing already—it's only a bruise."

So they began living in their new home—in which, as always happens, when they got thoroughly settled in they found they were just one room short—and with the increased income, which as always was just a little (about five hundred rubles) too little, but it was all very nice.

Things went particularly well at first, before everything was finally arranged and while something had still to be done: this thing bought, that thing ordered, another thing moved, and something else adjusted. Though there were some disputes between husband and wife, they were both so well satisfied and had so much to do that it all passed off without any serious quarrels. When nothing was left to arrange it became rather dull and something seemed to be lacking, but then they were making acquaintances, forming habits, and life was growing fuller.

Ivan Ilych spent his mornings at the law court and came home to dinner; at first he was generally in a good humor, though he occasionally became irritable just on account of his house. (Every spot on the tablecloth or the upholstery, and every broken window-blind string, irritated him. He had devoted so much trouble to arranging it all that every disturbance distressed him.) But on the whole his life ran its course as he believed life should do: easily, pleasantly, and decorously.

He got up at nine, drank his coffee, read the paper, and then put on his uniform and went to the law courts. There the harness in which he worked had already been stretched to fit him and he donned it without a hitch: petitioners, inquiries at the chancery, the chancery itself, and the sittings, both public and administrative. In all this the thing was to exclude everything fresh and vital, which always disturbs the regular course of official business, and to admit only official relations with people, and then only on official grounds. A man would come, for instance, wanting some information. Ivan Ilych, as one in whose sphere the matter did not lie, would have nothing to do with him: but if the man had some business with him in his official capacity, something that could be expressed on officially stamped paper, he would do everything, positively everything he could within the limits of such relations, and in doing so would maintain the semblance of friendly human relations, that is, would observe the courtesies of life. As soon as the official relations ended, so did everything else. Ivan Ilych possessed this capacity to separate his real life from the official side of affairs and not mix the two, in the highest degree, and by long practice and natural aptitude had brought it to such a pitch that sometimes, in the manner of a virtuoso, he would even allow himself to let the human and official relations mingle. He let himself do this just because he felt that at any time he could resume the strictly official attitude again and drop the human relation. And he did it all easily, pleasantly, correctly, even artistically. In the intervals between the sessions he smoked, drank tea, chatted a little about politics, a little about general topics, a little about cards, but most of all about official appointments. Tired, but feeling like a virtuoso—one of the first violins who has played his part in an orchestra with precision—he would return home to find that his wife and daughter had been out paying calls, or had a visitor, and that his son had been to school, had done his homework with his tutor, and was duly learning what is taught at High Schools. Everything was as it should be. After dinner, if they had no visitors, Ivan Ilych sometimes read a book that was being widely discussed at the time, and in the evening settled down to work, that is, read official papers, compared the depositions of witnesses, and noted paragraphs of the Code applying to them. This was neither dull nor amusing. It was dull when he might have been playing bridge, but if no bridge was available it was certainly better than doing nothing or sitting with his wife. Ivan Ilych's chief pleasure was giving little dinners to which he invited men and women of good social position, and just as his drawing-room resembled all other drawing-rooms so did his enjoyable little parties resemble all other parties.

Once they even gave a dance. Ivan Ilych enjoyed it and everything went off well, except that it led to a violent quarrel with his wife about the cakes and sweets. Praskovya Fedorovna had made her own plans, but Ivan Ilych insisted on getting everything from an expensive confectioner and ordered too many cakes. The quarrel occurred because some of those cakes were left over and the confectioner's bill came to forty-five rubles. It was a great and disagreeable quarrel. Praskovya Fedorovna called him "a fool and an imbecile," and he clutched at his head and made angry allusions to divorce.

But the dance itself had been enjoyable. The best people were there, and Ivan Ilych had danced with Princess Trufonova, a sister of the distinguished founder of the Society "Bear My Grief."[11]

The pleasures connected with his work were pleasures of ambition; his social pleasures were those of vanity; but Ivan Ilych's greatest pleasure was playing bridge. He acknowledged that whatever disagreeable incident happened in his life, the pleasure that beamed like a ray of sunshine above everything else was to sit down to bridge with good players, not noisy partners, and of course to four-handed bridge (with five players it was annoying to have to stand out, though one pretended not to mind), to play a clever and serious game (when the cards allowed it) and then to have supper and drink a glass of wine. After a game of bridge, especially if he had won a little (to win a large sum was unpleasant), Ivan Ilych went to bed in specially good humor.

So they lived. They formed a circle of acquaintances among the best people and were visited by people of importance and by young folk. In their views as to their acquaintances, husband, wife and daughter were entirely agreed, and tacitly and unanimously kept at arm's length and shook off various shabby friends and relations who, with much show of affection, gushed into the drawing-room with its Japanese plates on the walls. Soon these shabby friends ceased to obtrude themselves and only the best people remained in the Golovins' set.

Young men courted Lisa, and Petrishchev, an examining magistrate and Dmitri Ivanovich Petrishchev's son and sole heir, began to be so attentive to her that Ivan Ilych had already spoken to Praskovya Fedorovna about it, and considered whether they should not arrange a party for them, or organize some private theatricals.

So they lived, and all went well, without change, and life flowed pleasantly.

IV

They were all in good health. It could not be called ill health if Ivan Ilych sometimes said that he had a queer taste in his mouth and felt some discomfort in his left side.

But this discomfort increased and, though not exactly

painful, grew into a sense of pressure in his side accompanied by ill humor. His irritability became worse and worse and began to mar the agreeable, easy, and correct life that had established itself in the Golovin family. Quarrels between husband and wife became more and more frequent, and soon the ease and amenity disappeared and even the decorum was barely maintained. Once again scenes again became frequent, and very few issues remained on which husband and wife could meet without an explosion. Praskovya Fedorovna now had good reason to say that her husband's temper was trying. With characteristic exaggeration she said he had always had a dreadful temper, and that it had needed all her good nature to put up with it for twenty years. It was true that now their quarrels were started by him. His bursts of temper always came just before dinner, often just as he began to eat his soup. Sometimes he noticed that a plate or dish was chipped, or the food was not right, or his son put his elbow on the table, or his daughter's hair was not done as he liked it, and for all this he blamed Praskovya Fedorovna. At first she retorted and said disagreeable things to him, but once or twice he fell into such a rage at the beginning of dinner that she realized it was due to some physical derangement brought on by taking food, and so she restrained herself and did not answer, but only hurried to get through dinner. She regarded this self-restraint as highly praiseworthy. Having come to the conclusion that her husband had a dreadful temper and made her life miserable, she began to feel sorry for herself; the more she pitied herself the more she hated her husband. She began to wish he would die; yet she did not want him to die because then his salary would cease. And this irritated her still more. She considered herself dreadfully unhappy just because not even his death could save her, and though she concealed her exasperation, that hidden emotion of hers increased his irritation also.

After one scene in which Ivan Ilych had been particularly unfair and after which he had said in explanation that he certainly was irritable but that it was due to his not being well, she said that if he was ill it should be attended to, and insisted on his going to see a celebrated doctor.

He went. Everything took place as he had expected and as it always does. There was the usual waiting and the important air assumed by the doctor, with which he was so familiar (resembling that which he himself assumed in court), and the sounding and listening, and the questions which called for answers that were foregone conclusions and were evidently unnecessary, and the look of importance which implied that "if only you put yourself in our hands we will arrange everything—we know indubitably how it has to be done, always the same for everybody." It was all just as it was in the law courts. The doctor put on just the same air towards him as he himself put on towards an accused person.

The doctor said that so-and-so indicated that there was such-and-such inside the patient, but if the investigation of so-and-so did not confirm this, then he must assume this and that. If he assumed this and that, then . . . and so on. To Ivan Ilych only one question was important: was his case serious or not? But the doctor ignored that inappropriate question. From his point of view it was not the one under consideration; the real question was to decide between a floating kidney, chronic catarrh, or appendicitis. It was not a question of Ivan Ilych's life or death, but one between a floating kidney and appendicitis. And that question the doctor solved brilliantly, as it seemed to Ivan Ilych, in favor of the appendix, with the reservation that should an examination of his urine give fresh indications, the matter would be reconsidered. All this was just what Ivan Ilych had himself brilliantly accomplished a thousand times in dealing with men on trial. The doctor summed up just as brilliantly, looking over his spectacles triumphantly and even gaily at the accused. From the doctor's summation Ivan Ilych concluded that things were bad, but that for the doctor, and perhaps for everybody else, it was a matter of indifference, though for him it was bad. This conclusion struck him painfully, arousing in him a great feeling of pity for himself and of bitterness towards the doctor's indifference to a matter of such importance.

He said nothing about it, but rose, placed the doctor's fee on the table, and remarked with a sigh: "We sick people probably pose inappropriate questions frequently. But tell me, doctor, in general, is this complaint dangerous, or not? . . ."

The doctor looked at him sternly over his spectacles with one eye, as if to say: "Prisoner, if you will not keep to the questions put to you, I shall be obliged to have you removed from the court."

"I have already told you what I consider necessary and proper. The analysis may show something more." And the doctor bowed.

Ivan Ilych went out slowly, seated himself disconsolately in his sleigh, and drove home. All the way home he was going over what the doctor had said, trying to translate those complicated, obscure, scientific phrases into plain language and find in them an answer to the question: "Is my condition bad? Is it very bad? Or is there still nothing much wrong?" It seemed to him that the meaning of what the doctor had said was that it was very bad. Everything in the streets seemed depressing. The cabmen, the houses, the passers-by, and the shops, were dismal. His ache, this dull gnawing ache that never ceased for a moment, seemed to have acquired a new and more serious significance from the doctor's dubious remarks. Ivan Ilych now watched it with a new and oppressive feeling.

He reached home and began to tell his wife about it. She listened, but in the middle of his account his daughter came in with her hat on, ready to go out with her mother. She sat down reluctantly to listen to his tedious story, but could not stand it for very long, and her mother too did not hear him out to the end.

"Well, I'm very glad," she said. "Mind now to take your medicine regularly. Give me the prescription and I'll send Gerasim out to the pharmacy." And she went to get ready to go out.

While she was in the room Ivan Ilych had hardly taken time to breathe, but he sighed deeply when she left.

"Well," he thought, "perhaps it isn't so bad after all."

He began taking his medicine and following his doctor's orders, which had been altered after the examination of his urine. But then it seemed that there was a contradiction between the indications drawn from the examination of his urine and the symptoms that showed themselves. It turned out that what was happening differed from what the doctor had told him, and that he had either forgotten, or blundered, or hidden something from him. He could not, however, be blamed for that, and Ivan Ilych still obeyed his orders implicitly and at first derived some comfort from doing so.

From the time of his visit to the doctor, Ivan Ilych's chief occupation was the exact fulfillment of his doctor's instructions regarding hygiene and the taking of medicine, and the observation of his pain and his excretions. His chief interests came to be people's ailments and their health. When sickness, deaths, or recoveries were mentioned in his presence, especially when the illness resembled his own, he listened with considerable agitation which he tried to conceal, asked questions, and applied what he heard to his own case.

The pain did not diminish, but Ivan Ilych made efforts to force himself to think that he was better. He could do this so long as nothing agitated him. But as soon as he had any unpleasantness with his wife, any lack of success in his official work, or held bad cards at bridge, he was at once acutely aware of his disease. He had formerly borne such mishaps, hoping soon to adjust what was wrong, to master it and attain success, or make a grand slam. But now every mishap upset him and plunged him into despair. He would say to himself: "There now, just as I was beginning to get better and the medicine had begun to take effect, comes this accursed misfortune, or unpleasantness . . ." And he was furious with the mishap, or with the people who were causing the unpleasantness, for he felt that this fury was killing him but he could not restrain it. One would have thought that it should have been clear to him that this exasperation with circumstances and people aggravated his illness, and that therefore he ought to ignore unpleasant occurrences. But he drew the very opposite conclusion: he said that he needed peace, and he watched for everything that might disturb it and became irritable at the slightest infringement. His condition was rendered worse by the fact that he read medical books and consulted doctors. The progress of his disease was so gradual that he could deceive himself when comparing one day with another—the difference was so slight. But when he consulted the doctors it seemed to him that he was getting worse, even very rapidly. Yet despite this he was continually consulting them.

That month he went to see another celebrity, who told him almost the same as the first had done, but put his questions rather differently, and the interview with this celebrity only increased Ivan Ilych's doubts and fears. A friend of a friend of his, a very good doctor, diagnosed his illness again quite differently from the others, and though he predicted recovery, his questions and suppositions bewildered Ivan Ilych still more and increased his doubts. A homeopathist diagnosed the disease in yet another way, and prescribed medicine which Ivan Ilych took secretly for a week. But after this week, not feeling any improvement and having lost confidence both in the former doctor's treatment and in this one's, he became still more despondent. One day a lady acquaintance mentioned a cure effected by a wonder-working icon. Ivan Ilych caught himself listening attentively and beginning to believe that it had occurred. This incident alarmed him. "Has my mind really weakened to such an extent?" he asked himself. "Nonsense! It's all rubbish. I mustn't give way to nervous fears; having chosen a doctor must keep strictly to his treatment. That is what I will do. Now it's all settled. I won't think about it, but will follow the treatment seriously till summer, and then we shall see. From now on there must be no more wavering!" This was easy to say but impossible to carry out. The pain in his side oppressed him and seemed to grow worse and more incessant, while the taste in his mouth grew stranger and stranger. It seemed to him that his breath had a disgusting smell, and he was conscious of a loss of appetite and strength. There was no deceiving himself: something terrible, new, and more important than anything before in his life, was taking place within him of which he alone was aware. Those about him did not understand or would not understand it, but thought everything in the world was going on as usual. That tormented Ivan Ilych more than anything. He saw that his household, especially his wife and daughter who were in a perfect whirl of visiting, did not understand anything about it and were annoyed that he was so depressed and so exact-ing, as if he were to blame. Though they tried to disguise it he saw that he was an obstacle in their path, and that his wife had adopted a definite line in regard to his illness and kept to it regardless of anything he said or did. Her attitude was this: "You know," she would say to her friends, "Ivan Ilych can't do as other people do, and keep to the treatment prescribed for him. One day he takes his drops and keeps strictly to his diet and goes to bed in good time, but the next day unless I watch him, he suddenly forgets his medicine, eats sturgeon—which is forbidden—and sits up playing cards till one in the morning."

"Oh, come, when was that?" Ivan Ilych would ask in vexation. "Only once at Peter Ivanovich's."

"And yesterday with Shebek."

"Well, even if I hadn't stayed up, the pain would have kept me awake."

"Be that as it may you'll never get well like that, but you'll always make us wretched."

Praskovya Fedorovna's attitude to Ivan Ilych's illness, as she expressed it both to others and to him, was that it was all his own fault and was yet another of the annoyances he caused her. Ivan Ilych felt that this opinion escaped her in-voluntarily—but that did not make it any easier for him.

At the law courts too, Ivan Ilych noticed, or thought he noticed, a strange attitude towards himself. It sometimes seemed that people were watching him inquisitively as a man whose place might soon become vacant. Then again, his friends would suddenly begin to tease him in a friendly way about his low spirits, as if the awful, horrible, and unheard-of thing that was going on within him, incessantly gnawing at him and irresistibly drawing him away, was a very agreeable subject for jests. Schwartz in particular irritated him by his jocularity, vivacity, and *savoir-faire*, which reminded him of what he himself had been ten years ago.

Friends came to make up a set and they sat down to cards. They dealt, bending the new cards to soften them, and he sorted the diamonds in his hand and found he had seven. His partner said "No trumps" and supported him with two diamonds. What more could be wished for? It ought to be jolly and lively. They would make a grand slam. But suddenly Ivan Ilych was conscious of that gnawing pain, that taste in his mouth, and it seemed ridiculous that in such circumstances he should be pleased to make a grand slam.

He looked at his partner Mikhail Mikhailovich, who rapped the table with his strong hand and instead of snatching up the tricks pushed the cards courteously and indulgently towards Ivan Ilych that he might have the pleasure of gathering them up without the trouble of stretching out his hand for them. "Does he think I'm too weak to stretch out my arm?" thought Ivan Ilych, and forgetting what he was doing he over-trumped his partner, missing the grand slam by three tricks. And what was most awful of all was that he saw how upset Mikhail Mikhailovich was about it, but he himself did not care. And it was dreadful to realize why he did not care.

They all saw that he was suffering, and said: "We can stop if you're tired. Take a rest." Lie down? No, he was not tired at all, and finished the rubber. All were gloomy and silent. Ivan Ilych felt that he had diffused this gloom over them and was unable to dispel it. They had supper and went away; Ivan Ilych was left alone with the consciousness that his life was poisoned and was poisoning the lives of others, and that this poison did not lessen but penetrated more and more deeply into his whole being.

With this consciousness, and with physical pain besides the terror, he must go to bed, often to lie awake the greater part of the night. The next morning he had to get up again, dress, go to the law courts, speak, and write; or if he did not go out, spend those twenty-four hours a day at home each of which was a torture. And he had to live thus all alone on the brink of an abyss, with no one who understood him or pitied him.

V

So one month passed and then another. Just before the New Year his brother-in-law came to town and stayed at their house. Ivan Ilych was at the law courts and Praskovya Fedorovna had gone shopping. When Ivan Ilych came home and entered his study he found his brother-in-law there—a healthy, florid man—unpacking his bag himself. He raised his head on hearing Ivan Ilych's footsteps and looked up at him for a moment without a word. That stare told Ivan Ilych everything. His brother-in-law opened his mouth to

he would revert to when his work was done—never left him. When he had finished his work he remembered that this intimate matter was the thought of his vermiform appendix. But he did not give himself up to it, and went to the drawing-room for tea. There were callers there, including the examining magistrate who was a desirable match for his daughter, and they were conversing, playing the piano, and singing. Ivan Ilych, as Praskovya Fedorovna remarked, spent that evening more cheerfully than usual, but he never forgot for a moment that he had postponed the important matter of his appendix. At eleven o'clock he said good-night and went to his bedroom. Since his illness he had slept alone in a small room next to his study. He undressed and took up a novel by Zola, but instead of reading it he fell into thought, and in his imagination that desired improvement in the vermiform appendix occurred. There took place the absorption and evacuation and the re-establishment of normal activity. "Yes, that's it!" he said to himself. "One need only assist nature, that's all." He remembered his medicine, got up, took it, and lay down on his back waiting for the beneficent action of the medicine and for it to lessen the pain. "I need only take it regularly and avoid all injurious influences. I'm feeling better already, much better." He began touching his side: it was not painful to the touch. "There, I really don't feel it. It's much better already." He put out the light and turned over on his side . . . "My appendix is getting better, absorption is occurring." Suddenly he felt the old, familiar, dull, gnawing pain, stubborn and serious. There was the same familiar loathsome taste in his mouth. His heart sank and he felt dazed. "My God! My God!" he muttered. "Again, again! It will never cease." Suddenly the matter presented itself in quite a different aspect. "Vermiform appendix! Kidney!" he said to himself. "It's not a question of my appendix or my kidney, but of life and . . . death. Yes, life was there and now it is going, going and I cannot stop it. Yes. Why deceive myself? Isn't it obvious to everyone but me that I'm dying, and that it's only a question of weeks, days . . . it may happen any moment. There was light and now there's darkness. I was here and now I'm going there! Where?" A chill came over him, his breathing ceased, and he felt only the throbbing of his heart.

"When I'm not, what will there be? There'll be nothing. Then where will I be when I'm no more? Can this be dying? No, I don't want to!" He jumped up and tried to light the candle, felt for it with his trembling hands, dropped both candle and candlestick on the floor, and fell back on his pillow.

"What's the use? It makes no difference," he said to himself, staring with wide-open eyes into the darkness. "Death. Yes, death. And none of them knows or wishes to know it, and they have no pity for me. Now they are singing and playing." (He heard through the door the distant sound of a song and its accompaniment.) "It's all the same to them, but they'll die too! Fools! First me, and later them, but it'll be the same for them. And now they're merry . . . the beasts!"

Anger choked him and he was agonizingly, unbearably

miserable. "It's impossible that all men have been doomed to suffer this awful horror!" He raised himself up.

"Something must be wrong. I must calm myself—I must think it all over from the beginning." He began thinking again. "Yes, the beginning of my illness: I bumped my side, but I was still quite well that day and the next. It hurt a little, then rather more. I saw doctors, then followed despondency and anguish, more doctors, and I drew nearer to the abyss. My strength grew less and I kept coming nearer and nearer; now I have wasted away and there is no light left in my eyes. I think about my appendix—but this is really death! I think of mending my appendix, and all the while here comes death! Can it really be death?" Terror seized him again and he gasped for breath. He leant down and began feeling for the matches, pressing on the stand beside the bed with his elbow. It was in his way and it hurt him, he grew furious with it, pressed on it still harder, and upset it. Breathless and in despair he fell on his back, expecting death to come immediately.

Meanwhile the visitors were leaving. Praskovya Fedorovna was seeing them off. She heard something fall and came in.

"What happened?"

"Nothing. I knocked it over accidentally."

She went out and returned with a candle. He lay there panting heavily, like a man who's run a thousand yards, and stared at her with a fixed look.

"What is it, Jean?"

"No . . . o . . . thing. I knocked it over." ("Why speak about it? She won't understand," he thought.)

Indeed she did not understand. She picked up the stand, lit his candle, and hurried away to see another visitor off. When she came back he still lay on his back, looking upwards.

"What is it? Do you feel worse?"

"Yes."

She shook her head and sat down.

"Do you know, Jean, I think we must ask Leshchetitsky to come and see you here."

This meant calling in the famous specialist, regardless of expense. He smiled malignantly and said "No." She stayed a little longer and then went up to him and kissed his forehead.

While she was kissing him he hated her from the bottom of his heart and refrained with difficulty from pushing her away.

"Good-night. I pray to God you'll get some sleep."

"Yes."

VI

Ivan Ilych saw that he was dying, and he was in continual despair.

In the depth of his heart he knew he was dying, but not only was he unaccustomed to the thought, he simply did not and could not grasp it.

The syllogism he had learnt from Kiesewetter's Logic: "Caius is a man, men are mortal, therefore Caius is mortal,"[12] had always seemed to him correct as applied to Caius, but it certainly didn't apply to himself. That Caius—man in the abstract—was mortal, was perfectly correct, but he was not Caius, not an abstract man, but a creature quite separate from all others. He had been little Vanya, with a mamma and a papa, with Mitya and Volodya, with toys, a coachman and a nanny, afterwards with Katenka and with all the joys, griefs, and delights of childhood, boyhood, and youth. What did Caius know of the smell of that striped leather ball Vanya had been so fond of? Had Caius kissed his mother's hand like that, and did the silk of her dress rustle for Caius? Had he rioted like that at school when the pastry was bad? Had Caius been in love like that? Could Caius preside at a session as he did? "Caius really was mortal, and it was right for him to die; but as for me, little Vanya, Ivan Ilych, with all my thoughts and emotions, it's altogether a different matter. It cannot be that I ought to die. That would be too terrible."

Such was his feeling.

"If I had to die like Caius I should have known it. An inner voice would have told me so, but there was nothing of the sort in me; I and all my friends felt that our case was quite different from that of Caius. And now here it is!" he said to himself. "It can't be. It's impossible! But here it is. How's this? How's one to understand it?"

He could not understand it, and tried to drive away this false, incorrect, morbid thought and to replace it by other proper, healthy thoughts. But that thought, and not only the thought but the reality itself, seemed to come and confront him.

To replace that thought he called up a succession of others, hoping to find some support in them. He tried to get back into the former current of thoughts that had once screened the thought of death from him. But strange to say, all that had formerly shut off, hidden, and destroyed his consciousness of death, no longer had that effect. Ivan Ilych now spent most of his time attempting to re-establish that old current. He would say to himself: "I will take up my duties again—after all I used to live by them." Banishing all doubts he would go to the law courts, enter into conversation with his colleagues, and sit carelessly as was his wont, scanning the crowd with a thoughtful look and leaning both his emaciated arms on the arms of his oak chair; bending over as usual to a colleague and drawing his papers nearer he would exchange whispers with him, and then suddenly raising his eyes and sitting erect would pronounce certain words and open the proceedings. But suddenly in the midst of those proceedings the pain in his side, regardless of the stage the proceedings had reached, would begin its own gnawing work. Ivan Ilych would turn his attention to it and try to drive the thought of it away, but without success. *It* would come and stand before him and look at him, and he would be petrified. The light would die out in his eyes, and he would begin again asking himself whether *It* alone was true. His colleagues and subordinates would notice with surprise and distress that he, the brilliant and subtle judge, was becoming confused and making mistakes. He would shake himself, try to pull himself together, somehow manage to bring the session to a close, and return home with the sorrowful consciousness that his judicial labors could no longer hide from him what he wanted them to hide, and could not deliver him from *It*. And what was worst of all was that *It* drew his attention to itself not in order to make him take some action, but only so that he should look at *It*, look it straight in the face: look at it and without doing anything, suffer inexpressibly.

To save himself from this condition Ivan Ilych looked for consolations—new screens—and they were found and for a while seemed to save him, but then they immediately fell to pieces or rather became transparent, as if *It* penetrated them and nothing could veil *It*.

During these last few days he would go into the drawing-room he had arranged—that drawing-room where he had fallen and for the sake of which (how bitterly ridiculous it seemed) he had sacrificed his life—for he knew that his illness originated with that knock. He would enter and see that something had scratched the polished table. He would look for the cause and find that it was the bronze ornament on an album, that had got bent. He would take up the expensive album which he had lovingly arranged, and feel vexed with his daughter and her friends for their untidiness—the album was torn here and there and some of the photographs were turned upside down. He would put it carefully in order and bend the ornament back into position. Then it would occur to him to place all those things in another corner of the room, near the plants. He would call the footman, but his daughter or wife would come to help him. They wouldn't agree, and his wife would contradict him; he would dispute and grow angry. But that was all right, for then he didn't think about *It*. *It* was invisible.

But then, when he was moving something himself, his wife would say: "Let the servants do it. You'll hurt yourself again." Suddenly *It* would flash through the screen and he would see it. It was just a flash, and he hoped it would disappear, but involuntarily he would pay attention to his side. "It just sits there as before, gnawing just the same!" He could no longer forget *It*, but could see it distinctly looking at him from behind the flowers. "What's it all for?"

"It really is so! I lost my life over that curtain as I might have done storming a fort. Is that possible? How terrible and how stupid. It can't be true! It can't, but it is."

He would go to his study, lie down, and be alone again with *It*: face to face with *It*. Nothing could be done with *It* except to look at it and shudder.

VII

How it happened it is impossible to say because it came about step by step, unnoticed, but in the third month of Ivan Ilych's illness, his wife, his daughter, his son, his acquaintances, the doctors, the servants, and above all he himself, were aware that the whole interest he had for other people was whether he would soon vacate his place, and at last release the living from the discomfort caused by his presence and be released himself from his sufferings.

He slept less and less. He was given opium and hypodermic injections of morphine, but this did not relieve his pain. The dull depression he experienced in a somnolent condition at first gave him a little relief, but only as something new; afterwards it became as distressing as the pain itself or even more so.

Special foods were prepared for him on the doctors' orders, but all those foods became increasingly distasteful and disgusting to him.

For his excretions special arrangements had to be made, and this was a torment to him every time—a torment from the uncleanliness, the unseemliness, and the smell, and from knowing that another person had to take part in it.

But it was just through this most unpleasant matter, that Ivan Ilych obtained some comfort. Gerasim, the butler's young assistant, always came to carry things out. Gerasim was a clean, fresh peasant lad, grown stout on town food, always cheerful and bright. At first the sight of him, in his clean Russian peasant costume, engaged on such a disgusting task embarrassed Ivan Ilych.

Once when he got up from the commode too weak to draw up his own trousers, he dropped into a soft armchair and looked with horror at his bare, enfeebled thighs with the muscles so sharply marked on them.

Gerasim with a firm light tread, his heavy boots emitting a pleasant smell of tar and fresh winter air, came in wearing a clean Hessian apron, the sleeves of his print shirt tucked up over his strong bare young arms; refraining from looking at his sick master out of consideration for his feelings, and restraining the joy of life that beamed from his face, he went up to the commode.

"Gerasim!" said Ivan Ilych in a weak voice.

Gerasim started, evidently afraid he might have committed some blunder, and with a rapid movement turned his fresh, kind, simple young face which just showed the first downy signs of a beard.

"Yes, sir?"

"That must be very unpleasant for you. You must forgive me. I am helpless."

"Oh, why, sir," Gerasim's eyes beamed and he showed his glistening white teeth, "what's a little trouble? It's a case of illness with you, sir."

His deft strong hands did their accustomed task, and he went out of the room stepping lightly. Five minutes later he returned as lightly.

Ivan Ilych was still sitting in the same position in the armchair.

"Gerasim," he said when the latter had replaced the freshly-washed item. "Please come here and help me." Gerasim went up to him. "Lift me up. It is hard for me to get up, and I have sent Dmitri away."

Gerasim went up to him, grasped his master with his strong arms deftly but gently, in the same way that he moved—lifted him, supported him with one hand, and with the other drew up his trousers and would have set him down again, but Ivan Ilych asked to be led to the sofa. Gerasim, without effort and without apparent pressure, led him, almost lifting him, to the sofa and placed him on it.

"Thank you. How easily and well you do it all!"

Gerasim smiled again and turned to leave the room. But Ivan Ilych felt his presence such a comfort that he did not want to let him go.

"One thing more, please move up that chair. No, the other one—under my feet. It's easier for me when my feet are raised."

Gerasim brought the chair, set it down gently in place, and raised Ivan Ilych's legs on to it. It seemed to Ivan Ilych that he felt better while Gerasim was holding up his legs.

"It's better when my legs are higher," he said. "Place that cushion under them."

Gerasim did so. Again he lifted the legs and placed them, and again Ivan Ilych felt better while Gerasim held his legs. When he set them down Ivan Ilych fancied he felt worse.

"Gerasim," he said. "Are you busy now?"

"Not at all, sir," said Gerasim, who had learnt from townspeople how to speak to gentlefolk.

"What have you still to do?"

"What have I to do? I've done everything except chop the logs for tomorrow."

"Then hold my legs up a bit higher, will you?"

"Of course I will. Why not?" Gerasim raised his master's legs higher and Ivan Ilych thought that in that position he did not feel any pain at all.

"How about the logs?"

"Don't worry about that, sir. There's plenty of time."

Ivan Ilych told Gerasim to sit down and hold his legs, and began to talk to him. Strange to say it seemed that he felt better while Gerasim held his legs up.

After that Ivan Ilych would sometimes call Gerasim and get him to hold his legs on his shoulders, and he liked talking to him. Gerasim did it all easily, willingly, simply, and with good humor that touched Ivan Ilych. Health, strength, and vitality in other people were offensive to him, but Gerasim's strength and vitality did not mortify, but soothed him.

What tormented Ivan Ilych most was the deception, the lie, which for some reason they all accepted, that he was not dying but was simply ill, and that he need only keep still and undergo treatment and then something very good would result. He knew however that do what they would nothing would come of it, only still more agonizing suffering and death. This deception tortured him—their not wishing to admit what they all knew and what he knew, but wanting to lie to him concerning his terrible condition, and wishing and forcing him to participate in that lie. Those lies—enacted over him on the eve of his death and destined to degrade this awful, solemn act to the level of their visits, their curtains, their sturgeon for dinner—were a terrible agony for Ivan Ilych. And strangely enough, many times when they were going through their antics over him he had been within a hairbreadth of calling out to them: "Stop lying! You know and I know that I'm dying. Then at least stop lying about it!" But he had never the courage to do it. The awful, terrible act of his dying was, he could see, reduced by those around him to the level of a casual, unpleasant, almost indecorous incident (as if someone entered a drawing-room diffusing an unpleasant odor) and this was done by that very decorum which he had served his whole life long. He saw that no one felt for him, because no one even wished to grasp his position. Only Gerasim recognized it and pitied him. And so Ivan Ilych felt at ease only with him. He felt comforted when Gerasim supported his legs (sometimes all night long) and refused to go to bed, saying: "Don't you worry, Ivan Ilych. I'll get sleep enough later on," or when he suddenly became familiar and exclaimed: "If you weren't sick it would be another matter, but as it is, why should I grudge a little trouble?" Only Gerasim did not lie; everything showed that he alone understood the facts of the case and did not consider it necessary to disguise them, but simply felt sorry for his emaciated and enfeebled master. Once when Ivan Ilych was sending him away he even said straight out: "We shall all die, so why should I grudge a little trouble?"—expressing the fact that he did not consider his work burdensome, because he was doing it for a dying man and hoped someone would do the same for him when his time came.

Apart from this lying, or because of it, what tormented Ivan Ilych most was that no one pitied him as he wished to be pitied. At certain moments after prolonged suffering he wished most of all (though he would have been ashamed to confess it) for someone to pity him as a sick child is pitied. He longed to be petted and comforted. He knew he was an important functionary, that his beard was turning grey, and that therefore what he longed for was impossible, but still he longed for it. In Gerasim's attitude towards him there was something akin to what he wished for, and so that attitude comforted him. Ivan Ilych wanted to weep, wanted to be petted and cried over; then his colleague Shebek would come, and instead of weeping and being petted, Ivan Ilych would assume a serious, severe, and profound air. By force of habit he would express his opinion on a decision of the Court of Cassation[13] and would stubbornly insist on that view. This falsity around him and within him did more than anything else to poison his last days.

VIII

It was morning. He knew it was morning because Gerasim had gone, and Peter the footman had come in and put out the candles, drawn back one of the curtains, and quietly begun to tidy up. Whether it was morning or evening, Friday or Sunday, made no difference, it was all just the same: the gnawing, unmitigated, agonizing pain, never ceasing for an instant, the consciousness of life inexorably waning but not yet extinguished, the approach of that ever dreaded and hateful Death which was the only reality, and always the same falsity. What were days, weeks, hours, in such a case?

"Will you have some tea, sir?"

"He wants things to be regular, and wishes the gentlefolk to drink tea in the morning," thought Ivan Ilych, and only said "No."

"Wouldn't you like to move onto the sofa, sir?"

"He wants to tidy up the room, and I'm in the way. I am uncleanliness and disorder," he thought, and said only:

"No, leave me alone."

The man went on bustling about. Ivan Ilych stretched out his hand. Peter came up, ready to help.

"What is it, sir?"

"My watch."

Peter took the watch which was close at hand and gave it to his master.

"Half-past eight. Are they up?"

"No sir, except Vladimir Ivanovich" (the son) "who has gone to school. Praskovya Fedorovna ordered me to wake her if you asked for her. Shall I do so?"

"No, there's no need to." "Perhaps I'd better have some tea," he thought, and added aloud: "Yes, bring me some tea."

Peter went to the door, but Ivan Ilych dreaded being left alone. "How can I keep him here? Oh yes, my medicine." "Peter, give me my medicine." "Why not? Perhaps it may still do me some good." He took a spoonful and swallowed it. "No, it won't help. It's all foolishness, all deception," he decided as soon as he became aware of the familiar, sickly, hopeless taste. "No, I can't believe in it any longer. But the pain, why this pain? If it would only cease just for a moment!" And he moaned. Peter turned towards him. "It's all right. Go and fetch me some tea."

Peter went out. Left alone Ivan Ilych groaned not so much with pain, terrible though that was, as from mental anguish. Always and forever the same, always these endless days and nights. If only it would come quicker! If only *what* would come quicker? Death, darkness? . . . No, no! Anything rather than death!

When Peter returned with the tea on a tray, Ivan Ilych stared at him for a time in perplexity, not realizing who and what he was. Peter was disconcerted by that look and his embarrassment brought Ivan Ilych to himself.

"Oh, tea! All right, put it down. Only help me wash and put on a clean shirt."

Ivan Ilych began to wash. With pauses for rest, he washed his hands and then his face, cleaned his teeth, brushed his hair, and looked in the mirror. He was terrified by what he saw, especially by the limp way in which his hair clung to his pallid forehead.

While his shirt was being changed he knew that he would be still more frightened at the sight of his body, so he avoided looking at it. Finally he was ready. He drew on a dressing-gown, wrapped himself in a plaid, and sat down in the armchair to take his tea. For a moment he felt refreshed, but as soon as he began to drink the tea he was again aware of the same taste, and the pain returned too. He finished it with an effort, and then lay down stretching out his legs, and dismissed Peter.

Always the same. Now a spark of hope flashes up, then a sea of despair rages, and always pain; always pain, always despair, and always the same. When alone he had a dreadful and distressing desire to call someone, but he knew beforehand that with others present it would be still worse. "Another dose of morphine—to lose consciousness. I'll tell him, the doctor, that he must think of something else. It's impossible, impossible, to go on like this."

An hour and another pass like that. But now there's a ring at the door bell. Perhaps it's the doctor? It is. He comes in fresh, hearty, plump, and cheerful, with that look on his face that seems to say: "There now, you're in a panic about something, but we'll arrange it all for you at once!" The doctor knows this expression is out of place here, but he has put it on once and for all and can't take it off—like a man who has put on a frock-coat in the morning to pay a round of calls.

The doctor rubs his hands vigorously and reassuringly.

"Brr! How cold it is! There's such a sharp frost; just let me warm myself!" he says, as if it were only a matter of waiting till he was warm, and then he would put everything right.

"Well now, how are you?"

Ivan Ilych feels that the doctor would like to say: "Well, how are our affairs?" but that even he feels this would not do, and says instead: "What sort of a night did you have?"

Ivan Ilych looks at him as if to say: "Are you really never ashamed of lying?" But the doctor does not wish to understand this question, and Ivan Ilych says: "Just as terrible as ever. The pain never leaves me and never subsides. If only something . . ."

"Yes, you sick people are always like that. . . . There, now I think I'm warm enough. Even Praskovya Fedorovna, who's so particular, could find no fault with my temperature. Well, now I can say good-morning," and the doctor presses his patient's hand.

Then, dropping his former playfulness, he begins with a most serious face to examine the patient, feeling his pulse and taking his temperature, and then begins the sounding and auscultation.

Ivan Ilych knows quite well and definitely that this is all nonsense and pure deception, but when the doctor, getting down on his knee, leans over him, putting his ear first higher then lower, and performs various gymnastic movements over him with a significant expression on his face, Ivan Ilych submits to it all just as he used to submit to the speeches of the lawyers, though he knew very well that they were all lying and knew why they were lying.

The doctor, kneeling on the sofa, is still sounding him when Praskovya Fedorovna's silk dress rustles at the door and she's heard scolding Peter for not having let her know of the doctor's arrival.

She comes in, kisses her husband, and at once proceeds to prove that she has been up a long time, and owing only to a misunderstanding failed to be there when the doctor arrived.

Ivan Ilych looks at her, scans her all over, sets against her the whiteness, plumpness, and cleanness of her hands and neck, the gloss of her hair, and the sparkle of her vivacious eyes. He hates her with his whole soul. The thrill of hatred he feels for her makes him suffer from her touch.

Her attitude towards him and his disease is still the same.

Just as the doctor had adopted a certain relation to his patient which he could not abandon, so had she formed one towards him—that he was not doing something he ought to do and was himself to blame, and she reproached him lovingly for this—and now she could not change that attitude.

"You see he doesn't listen to me and doesn't take his medicine at the proper time. Above all he lies in a position that's no doubt bad for him—with his legs up."

She described how he made Gerasim hold his legs up.

The doctor smiled with a contemptuous affability that said: "What's to be done? These sick people do have foolish fancies of that kind, but we must forgive them."

When the examination was over the doctor looked at his watch, and then Praskovya Fedorovna announced to Ivan Ilych that it was of course as he pleased, but she had sent today for a celebrated specialist who would examine him and have a consultation with Mikhail Danilovich (their regular doctor).

"Please don't raise any objections. I'm doing this for my own sake," she said ironically, letting it be felt that she was doing it all for his sake and only said this to leave him no right to refuse. He remained silent, knitting his brows. He felt that he was surrounded and involved in such a mesh of falsity that it was hard to unravel anything.

Everything she did for him was entirely for her own sake; she told him she was doing for herself what she actually was doing for herself, as if that was so incredible he must understand the opposite.

At half-past eleven the celebrated specialist arrived. Again the sounding began and the significant conversations in his presence and in another room, about his kidneys and appendix, and the questions and answers, with such an air of importance that again, instead of the real question of life and death which now alone confronted him, the question arose of his kidney and appendix which were not behaving as they ought to and would now be attacked by Mikhail Danilovich and the specialist and forced to mend their ways.

The celebrated specialist took leave of him with a serious though not hopeless look, and in reply to the timid question Ivan Ilych, eyes glistening with fear and hope, put to him as to whether there was any chance of recovery, said that he could not vouch for it but there was a possibility. The look of hope with which Ivan Ilych watched the doctor out was so pathetic that Praskovya Fedorovna, seeing it, even wept as she left the room to hand the doctor his fee.

The gleam of hope kindled by the doctor's encouragement did not last long. The same room, the same pictures, curtains, wall-paper, medicine bottles, were all there, and the same aching suffering body, and Ivan Ilych began to moan. They gave him a subcutaneous injection and he sank into oblivion.

It was twilight when he came to. They brought him his dinner and he swallowed some beef broth with difficulty; then everything was the same again and night was coming on.

After dinner, at seven o'clock, Praskovya Fedorovna came into the room in evening dress, her full bosom pushed up by her corset, and with traces of powder on her face. She had reminded him in the morning that they were going to the theater. Sarah Bernhardt[14] was visiting the town and they had a box, which he had insisted on their taking. Now he had forgotten about it and her toilet offended him, but he concealed his vexation when he remembered that he had himself insisted on their securing a box and going because it would be an instructive and aesthetic pleasure for the children.

Praskovya Fedorovna came in, self-satisfied but with a rather guilty air. She sat down and asked how he was, but, as he saw, only for the sake of asking and not in order to learn about it, knowing that there was nothing to learn. Then she went on to what she really wanted to say: she would not on any account have gone but the box had been taken and Helen and their daughter were going, as well as Petrishchev (the examining magistrate, their daughter's fiancé) and that it was out of the question to let them go alone. She would have much preferred to sit with him for a while; he must be sure to follow the doctor's orders while she was away.

"Oh, and Fedor Petrovich" (the fiancé) "would like to come in. May he? And Lisa?"

"All right."

Their daughter came in in full evening dress, her fresh young flesh exposed (making a show of that very flesh which in his own case caused so much suffering), strong, healthy, evidently in love, and impatient with his illness, suffering, and death, because they interfered with her happiness.

Fedor Petrovich came in too, in evening dress, his hair curled *à la Capoul*,[15] a tight stiff collar around his long sinewy neck, an enormous white shirt-front and narrow black trousers tightly stretched over his strong thighs. He had one white glove tightly drawn on, and was holding his opera hat in his hand.

Following him the schoolboy crept in unnoticed, in a new uniform, poor little fellow, and wearing gloves. Terribly dark shadows showed under his eyes, the meaning of which Ivan Ilych knew well.

His son had always seemed pathetic to him, and now it was dreadful to see the boy's frightened look of pity. It seemed to Ivan Ilych that Vasya was the only one besides Gerasim who understood and pitied him.

They all sat down and again asked how he was. A silence followed. Lisa asked her mother about the opera-glasses, and there was an altercation between mother and daughter as to who had taken them and where they had been put. This occasioned some unpleasantness.

Fedor Petrovich inquired of Ivan Ilych whether he had ever seen Sarah Bernhardt. Ivan Ilych did not at first catch the question, but then replied: "No, have you seen her before?"

"Yes, in *Adrienne Lecouvreur*."[16]

Praskovya Fedorovna mentioned some roles in which Sarah Bernhardt was particularly good. Her daughter disagreed. Conversation sprang up as to the elegance and realism of her acting—the sort of conversation that is always repeated and is always the same.

In the midst of the conversation Fedor Petrovich glanced at Ivan Ilych and became silent. The others also looked at him and grew silent. Ivan Ilych was staring with glittering eyes straight before him, evidently indignant with them. This had to be rectified, but it was impossible to do so. The silence had to be broken, but for a time no one dared break it and they all became afraid that the conventional deception would suddenly become obvious and the truth become plain to all. Lisa was the first to pluck up her courage and break that silence, but by trying to hide what everybody was feeling, she betrayed it.

"Well, if we're going it's time to start," she said, looking at her watch, a present from her father, with a faint, significant smile at Fedor Petrovich relating to something known only to them. She got up with a rustle of her dress.

They all rose, said good-night, and went away.

When they had gone it seemed to Ivan Ilych that he felt better; the falsity had gone away with them. But the pain remained—the same pain and the same fear that made everything monotonously alike, nothing harder and nothing easier. Everything was worse.

Again minute followed minute and hour followed hour. Everything remained the same; there was no cessation. The inevitable end of it all became more and more terrible.

"Yes, send Gerasim in here," he replied to a question Peter asked.

IX

His wife returned late at night. She came in on tip-toe, but he heard her, opened his eyes, and made haste to close them again. She wished to send Gerasim away and sit with him herself, but he opened his eyes and said: "No, go away."

"Are you in great pain?"

"Always the same."

"Take some opium."

He agreed and took some. She went away.

Till about three in the morning he was in a state of stupefied misery. It seemed to him that he and his pain were being thrust into a narrow, deep black sack, and though they were being pushed further and further in they could not be pushed to the bottom. And this, terrible enough in itself, was accompanied by suffering. He was frightened, yet wanted to fall through the sack; he struggled yet co-operated. Suddenly he broke through, fell, and regained consciousness. Gerasim was sitting at the foot of the bed dozing quietly and patiently, while he himself lay with his emaciated stockinged legs resting on Gerasim's shoulders; the same shaded candle stood there and the same unceasing pain.

"Go away, Gerasim," he whispered.

"It's all right, sir. I'll stay a while."

"No. Go away."

He removed his legs from Gerasim's shoulders, turned sideways onto his arm, and felt sorry for himself. He only waited till Gerasim had gone into the next room and then restrained himself no longer but wept like a child. He wept on account of his helplessness, his terrible loneliness, the cruelty of man, the cruelty of God, and the absence of God.

"Why hast Thou done all this? Why hast Thou brought me here? Why, why dost Thou torment me so terribly?"

He did not expect an answer and wept because there was no answer and could be none. The pain grew more acute again, but he did not stir and did not call. He said to himself: "Go on! Strike me! But what is it for? What have I done to Thee? What is it for?"

Then he grew quiet and not only ceased weeping, but even held his breath and became all attention. It was as though he were listening not to an audible voice, but to the voice of his soul, to the current of thoughts arising within him.

"What do you want?" was the first clear conception capable of being expressed in words, that he heard.

"What do you want? What do you want?" he repeated to himself.

"What do I want? To live and not to suffer," he answered.

Again he listened with such concentrated attention that even his pain did not distract him.

"To live? How?" asked his inner voice.

"Why, to live as I used to—well and pleasantly."

"As you lived before, well and pleasantly?" the voice repeated.

And in his imagination he began to recall the best moments of his pleasant life. But strange to say none of those best moments of his pleasant life now seemed at all what they had seemed then—none of them except his first recollections of childhood. There, in childhood, there had been something really pleasant with which it would be possible to live, if it could return. But the child who had experienced that happiness no longer existed, it was like a recollection of somebody else.

As soon as the period began which had produced the present Ivan Ilych, all that had then seemed joys now melted away before his sight and turned into something trivial and often nasty.

The further he departed from childhood and the nearer he came to the present the more worthless and doubtful were the joys. This began with the School of Law. A little that was really good was still to be found there—there was light-heartedness, friendship, and hope. But in the upper classes there had already been fewer good moments. Then during the first years of his official career, when he was in the service of the governor, some pleasant moments occurred again: they were the memories of his love for a woman. Then all became confused and there was still less of what was good; later on again there was even less that was good, and the further he went the less there was. His marriage, a mere accident, then the disenchantment that followed it, his wife's bad breath and her sensuality and hypocrisy: then that deadly official life and those preoccupations about money, a year of it, two, ten, twenty, and always the same thing. The longer it lasted the more deadly it became. "It is as if I had been going downhill while I imagined I was going up. And that's really what it was. I was going up in public opinion, but to the same extent life was ebbing away from me. And now it's all over and there's only death.

"Then what does it mean? Why? It can't be that life is so senseless and horrible. But if it really has been so horrible and senseless, why must I die and die in agony? There's something wrong!

"Maybe I didn't live as I ought to have done," it suddenly occurred to him. "But how could that be, when I did everything properly?" he replied, and immediately dismissed from his mind this, the sole solution of all the riddles of life and death, as something quite impossible.

"Then what do you want now? To live? Live how? Live as you lived in the law courts when the usher proclaimed 'The judge is coming!' The judge is coming, the judge!" he repeated to himself. "Here he is, the judge. But I'm not guilty!" he exclaimed angrily. "What is it for?" And he ceased crying, but turning his face to the wall continued to ponder on the same question: Why, and for what purpose, is there all this horror? But however much he pondered, he found no answer. And whenever the thought occurred to him, as it often did, that it all resulted from his not having lived as he ought to have done, he recalled at once the correctness of his whole life and dismissed so strange an idea.

X

Another fortnight passed. Ivan Ilych now no longer left his sofa. He would not lie in bed but lay on the sofa, facing the wall nearly all the time. He suffered the same unceasing agonies and in his loneliness pondered the same insoluble question: "What is this? Can it be that it is Death?" And the inner voice answered: "Yes, it is Death."

"Why these sufferings?" And the voice answered, "For no reason—just so." Beyond and besides this, there was nothing.

From the very beginning of his illness, ever since he had first been to see the doctor, Ivan Ilych's life had been divided between two contrary and alternating moods: either despair and the expectation of this uncomprehended and terrible death, or hope and an intently interested observation of the functioning of his organs. Before his eyes there was either a kidney or an intestine that temporarily evaded its duty, or that incomprehensible and dreadful death from which it was impossible to escape.

These two states of mind had alternated from the very beginning of his illness, but the further it progressed, the more doubtful and fantastic became the conception of his kidney, and the more real the sense of impending death.

He had but to recall what he had been three months before and what he was now, to recall with what regularity he had been going downhill, for every possibility of hope to be shattered.

Lately during that loneliness in which he found himself as he lay facing the back of the sofa, a loneliness in the midst of a populous town, surrounded by numerous acquaintances and relations, but that could not have been more complete anywhere—either at the bottom of the sea or under the earth—during that terrible loneliness Ivan Ilych had lived only in memories of the past. Pictures of his past rose before him one after another. They always began with what was nearest in time and then went back to what was most remote—to his childhood—and stopped there. If he thought of the stewed prunes that had been offered him that day, his mind went back to the raw shrivelled French plums of his childhood, their peculiar flavor and the flow of saliva when he sucked their pits; along with the memory of that taste came a whole series of memories of those days: his nanny, his brother, and their toys. "No, I mustn't think of that. . . . It's too painful," Ivan Ilych said to himself, and brought himself back to the present—to the button on the back of the sofa and the creases in its morocco. "Morocco is expensive, but it doesn't wear well: there had been a quarrel about it. It was a different kind of quarrel and a different kind of morocco that time when we tore father's portfolio and were punished, and mamma brought us some tarts. . . ." Once again his thoughts dwelt on childhood; again it was painful and he tried to banish them and fix his mind on something else.

Then together with that chain of memories another series passed through his mind—of how his illness had progressed and grown worse. There too the further back he looked, the more life there was. There had been more of what was good in life and more of life itself. The two merged. "Just as the pain went on getting worse and worse, so my life grew worse and worse," he thought. "There's one bright spot there at the back, at the beginning of life, and afterwards all becomes blacker and blacker and proceeds more and more rapidly—in inverse ratio to the square of the distance from death," thought Ivan Ilych. And the example of a stone falling downwards with increasing velocity entered his mind. Life, a series of increasing sufferings, flies further and further towards its end—the most terrible suffering. "I'm flying. . . ." He shuddered, shifted himself, and tried to resist, but was already aware that resistance was impossible, and again with eyes tired of gazing but unable to cease seeing what was before them, he stared at the back of the sofa and waited—awaiting that dreadful fall and shock and destruction.

"Resistance is impossible!" he said to himself. "If I could only understand what it's all for! But that too is impossible. An explanation would be possible if it could be said that I've not lived as I ought to. But it's impossible to say that," and he remembered all the legality, correctitude, and propriety of his life. "At any rate that can certainly not be admitted," he thought, and his lips smiled ironically as if someone could see that smile and be taken in by it. "There's no explanation! Agony, death. . . .What for?"

XI

Another two weeks went by in this way and during that time an event occurred that Ivan Ilych and his wife had desired. Petrishchev formally proposed. It happened in the evening. The next day Praskovya Fedorovna came into her husband's room considering how best to inform him of it, but that very night there had been a change for the worse in his condition. She found him still lying on the sofa but in a different position. He lay on his back, groaning and staring fixedly straight in front of him.

She began to remind him about his medicines, but he turned his eyes towards her with such a look that she did not finish what she was saying; so great an animosity, to her in particular, did that look express.

"For Christ's sake let me die in peace!" he said.

She would have gone away, but just then their daughter came in and went to say good morning. He looked at her as he had his wife, and in reply to her inquiry about his health said dryly that he would soon free them all of himself. They were both silent and after sitting with him for a while went away.

"Is it our fault?" Lisa asked her mother. "It's as if we were to blame! I'm sorry for papa, but why should we be tortured?"

The doctor came at his usual time. Ivan Ilych answered "Yes" and "No," never taking his angry eyes from him, and said at last: "You know you can do nothing for me, so leave me alone."

"We can ease your sufferings."

"You can't even do that. Let me be."

The doctor went into the drawing-room and told Praskovya Fedorovna that the situation was very serious and that the only resource left was opium to allay her husband's sufferings, which must be terrible.

It was true, as the doctor said, Ivan Ilych's physical suf-ferings were terrible, but worse than the physical sufferings were his mental sufferings which were his chief torture.

His mental sufferings were due to the fact that that night, as he looked at Gerasim's sleepy, good-natured face with its prominent cheek-bones, the question suddenly occurred to him: "What if my whole life has been wrong?"

It occurred to him that what had appeared perfectly impossible before, namely that he had not spent his life as he should have done, might be true after all. It occurred to him that his scarcely perceptible attempts to struggle against what was considered good by the most highly placed people, those scarcely noticeable impulses which he had immedi-ately suppressed, might have been the real thing, and all the rest false. His professional duties and the whole arrangement of his life and his family, all his social and official interests, might all have been false. He tried to defend all those things to himself and suddenly felt the weakness of what he was defending. There was nothing to defend.

"But if that's so," he said to himself, "and I'm leaving this life with the consciousness that I've lost all that was given me and it's impossible to rectify it—what then?"

He lay on his back and began to pass his life in review in quite a new way. In the morning when he first saw his foot-man, then his wife, then his daughter, and then the doctor, their every word and movement confirmed the awful truth that had been revealed to him during the night. In them he saw himself—all that for which he had lived—and saw clearly that it was not real at all, but a terrible and huge deception which had hidden both life and death. This consciousness intensified his physical suffering tenfold. He groaned, tossed about, and pulled at his clothing which choked and stifled him. And he hated them on that account.

He was given a large dose of opium and became unconscious, but at noon his sufferings began again. He drove everybody away and tossed from side to side.

His wife came to him and said:

"Jean, my dear, do this for me. It can't do any harm and it often helps. Healthy people often do it."

He opened his eyes wide.

"What? Take communion? Why? It's unnecessary! However . . ."

She began to cry.

"Yes, do, my dear. I'll send for our priest. He's such a nice man."

"All right. Very well," he muttered.

When the priest came and heard his confession, Ivan Ilych was softened and seemed to feel some relief from his doubts and consequently from his sufferings, and for a moment there came a ray of hope. Again he began to think of his vermiform appendix and the possibility of correcting it. He received the sacrament with tears in his eyes.

When they laid him down again afterwards he felt a moment's peace, and the hope that he might live awoke in him once again. He began to think of the operation that had been suggested to him. "To live! I want to live!" he said to himself.

His wife came in to congratulate him after his communion, and when uttering the usual conventional words she added:

"You feel better, don't you?"

Without looking at her he said "Yes."

Her dress, her figure, the expression of her face, the tone of her voice, all revealed the same thing. "This is wrong, it's not as it should be. All you've lived for and still live for is falsehood and deception, hiding life and death from you." As soon as he admitted that thought, his hatred and agonizing physical suffering increased again, and with that suffering a consciousness of the unavoidable, approaching end. And to this was added a new sensation of grinding, shooting pain and a feeling of suffocation.

The expression of his face when he uttered that "Yes" was dreadful. Having uttered it, he looked her straight in the eyes, turned his face away with a rapidity extraordinary in his weak state and shouted:

"Go away! Go away and leave me alone!"

XII

From that moment the screaming began that continued for three days, and was so terrible that one could not hear it through two closed doors without horror. At the moment he answered his wife he realized that he was lost, that there was no return, that the end had come, the very end, and his doubts were still unsolved and remained doubts.

"Oh! Oh! Oh!" he cried in various intonations. He had

begun by screaming "I won't!" and continued screaming on the letter "O."

For three whole days, during which time did not exist for him, he struggled in that black sack into which he was being thrust by an invisible, irresistible force. He struggled as a man condemned to death struggles in the hands of the executioner, knowing that he cannot save himself. Every moment he felt that despite all his efforts he was drawing nearer and nearer to what terrified him. He felt that his agony was due to his being thrust into that black hole and still more to his not being able to get right into it. He was hindered from getting into it by his conviction that his life had been a good one. That very justification of his life held him fast and prevented his moving forward, and it caused him the most torment of all.

Suddenly some force struck him in the chest and side, making it even harder to breathe, and he fell through the hole and there at the bottom was a light. What had happened to him was like the sensation one sometimes experiences in a railway carriage when one thinks one is going backwards while one is really going forwards and suddenly becomes aware of the real direction.

"Yes, it was all not the right thing," he said to himself, "but that doesn't matter. The "right thing" can still be done. But what *is* the right thing?" he asked himself, and suddenly grew quiet.

This occurred at the end of the third day, two hours before his death. Just then his schoolboy son had crept in softly and gone up to the bedside. The dying man was still screaming desperately and waving his arms. His hand fell on the boy's head, and the boy caught it, pressed it to his lips, and began to cry.

At that very moment Ivan Ilych fell through and caught sight of the light, and it was revealed to him that though his life had not been what it should have been, it could still be rectified. He asked himself, "What *is* the right thing?" and grew still, listening. Then he felt that someone was kissing his hand. He opened his eyes, looked at his son, and felt sorry for him. His wife came up to him and he glanced at her. She was gazing at him open-mouthed, with undried tears on her nose and cheek and a despairing look on her face. He felt sorry for her too.

"Yes, I am making them all wretched," he thought. "They're sorry, but it'll be better for them when I die." He wished to say this, but didn't have the strength to utter it. "Besides, why speak? I must act," he thought. With a look at his wife he indicated his son and said:

"Take him away . . . sorry for him . . . and for you too. . . ." He tried to add, "Forgive me," but said "Let me through"[17] and waved his hand, knowing that He whose understanding mattered would understand.

Suddenly it grew clear to him that what had been oppressing him and would not leave him was all dropping away at once from two sides, from ten sides, from all sides. He was sorry for them, he must act so as not to hurt them: release them and free himself from these sufferings. "How good and how simple!" he thought. "And the pain?" he asked himself. "What has become of it? Where are you, pain?"

He turned his attention to it.

"Yes, here it is. Well, what of it? Let it be."

"And death . . . where is it?"

He looked for his former accustomed fear of death and did not find it. "Where is it? What death?" There was no fear because there was no death.

In place of death there was light.

"So that's what it is!" he suddenly exclaimed aloud. "What joy!"

To him all this happened in a single instant, and the meaning of that instant did not change. For those present his agony continued for another two hours. Something rattled in his throat, his emaciated body twitched, then the gasping and rattle became less and less frequent.

"It is finished!" said someone near him.

He heard these words and repeated them in his soul.

"Death is finished," he said to himself. "It is no more!"

He drew in a breath, stopped in the midst of a sigh, stretched out, and died.

ILYCH NOTES

This piece was first published in 1886.

1. The phoenix of the family.

2. Look to, or regard, the end (Lat.).

3. Old believers who rejected Patriarch Nikon's reforms in the mid-seventeenth century.

4. A good fellow.

5. Youth will have its fling.

6. As it should be, proper, fitting.

7. Major judicial reform that followed emancipation of the serfs in 1861.

8. A form of bridge.

9. Out of sheer wantonness.

10. Second wife of Paul I, Marya Fyodorovna was dowager empress during the reign of Alexander I (1801–25). She founded several charitable institutions and schools.

11. A charitable organization patronized by the empress.

12. J.G. Kiesewetter (1766–1819), a follower of Kant, published a textbook of logic widely used in Russian schools. Caius is Julius Caesar.

13. An appeals court for criminal cases, which was created by the judicial reform of 1864.

14. The famous French actress (1844–1923) was on tour in Russia during the winter of 1881–82.

15. Named after the French tenor Joseph Capoul (1839–1924), the hairstyle consisted of a part down the middle with a curl on each side of the forehead.

16. A comedy written by A.E. Scribe and E. Legouvé in 1849 based on the life of the eighteenth-century French actress. The title role was one of Sarah Bernhardt's most successful parts.

17. Ivan misspeaks: he means to say *Prosti* (Forgive me), but utter the word *Propusti* (Let me through) by mistake.

TILLIE OLSEN

TELL ME A RIDDLE

—

INTRO EX

For forty-seven years they had been married. How deep back the stubborn, gnarled roots of the quarrel reached, no one could say—but only now, when tending to the needs of others no longer shackled them together, the roots swelled up visible, split the earth between them, and the tearing shook even to the children, long since grown.

Why now, why now? Wailed Hannah.

As if when we grew up weren't enough, said Paul.

Poor Ma. Poor Dad. It hurts so for both of them, said Vivi. They never had very much; at least in old age they should be happy.

Knock their heads together, insisted Sammy; tell 'em: you're too old for this kind of thing; no reason not to get along now.

Lennie wrote to Clara: They lived over so much together; what could possibly tear them apart?

Something tangible enough.

Arithritic hands, and such work as he got, occasional. Poverty all his life, and there was little breath left for running. He could not, could not turn away from this desire: to have the troubling of responsibility, the fretting with money, over and done with; to be free, to be *care*free where success was not measured by accumulation, and there was use for the vitality still in him.

There was a way. They could sell the house, and with the money join his lodge's Haven, co-operative for the aged. Happy communal life, and was he not already an official; had he not helped organize it, raise funds, served as a trustee?

But she—would not consider it.

"What do we need all this for?" he would ask loudly, for her hearing aid was turned down and the vacuum was shrilling. "Five rooms" (pushing the sofa so she could get into the corner) "furniture" (smoothing down the rug) "floors and surfaces to make work. Tell me, why do we need it?" And he was glad he could ask in a scream.

"Because I'm use't." *routine*

"Because you're use't. This is a reason, Mrs. Word Miser? Used to can get unused!"

"Enough unused I have to get used to already. . . . Not enough words?" turning off the vacuum a moment to hear herself answer. "Because soon enough we'll need only a little closet, no windows, no furniture, nothing to make work for but worms. Because now I want a room. . . . Screech and blow like you're doing, you'll need that closet even sooner. . . . Ha, again!" for the vacuum bag wailed, puffed half up, hung stubbornly limp. "This time fix it so it stays; quick before the phone rings and you get too important-busy."

But while he struggled with the motor, it seethed in him. Why fix it? Why have to bother? And if it can't be fixed, have to wring the mind with how to pay for the repair? At the Haven they come in with their own machines to clean your room or your cottage; you fish, or play cards, or make jokes in the sun, not with knotty fingers fight to mend vacuums.

Over the dishes, coaxingly: "For once in your life, to be free, to have everything done for you, like a queen."

"I never liked queens."

"No dishes, no garbage, no towel to sop, no worry what to buy, what to eat."

"And what else would I do with my empty hands? Better to eat at my own table when I want, and to cook and eat how I want."

"In the cottages they buy what you ask, and cook it how you like it. *You* are the one who always used to say: better mankind born without mouths and stomachs than always to worry for money to buy, to shop, to fix, to cook, to wash, to clean."

"How cleverly you hid that you heard. I said it then because eighteen hours a day I ran. And you never scraped a carrot or knew a dish towel sops. Now—for you and me—who cares? A herring out of a jar is enough. But when

107

I want, and nobody to bother." And she turned off her ear button, so she would not have to hear.

differences

But as *he* had no peace, juggling and rejuggling the money to figure: how will I pay for this now?; prying out the storm windows (there they take care of this); jolting in the streetcar on errands (there I would not have to ride to take care of this or that); fending the patronizing relatives just back from Florida (there it matters what one is, not what one can afford), he gave *her* no peace.

"Look! In their bulletin. A reading circle. Twice a week it meets."

"Haumm," her answer of not listening.

"A reading circle. Chekhov they read that you like, and Peretz. Cultured people at the Haven that you would enjoy."

past view

"Enjoy!" She tasted the word. "Now, when it pleases you, you find a reading circle for me. And forty years ago when the children were morsels and there was a Circle, did you stay home with them once so I could go? Even once? You trained me well. I do not need others to enjoy. Others!" Her voice trembled. "Because *you* want to be there with others. Already it makes me sick to think of you always around others. Clown, grimacer, floormat, yesman, entertainer, whatever they want of you."

And now it was he who turned on the television loud so he need not hear.

Old scar tissue ruptured and the wounds festered anew. Chekhov indeed. She thought without softness of that young wife, who in the deep night hours while she nursed the current baby, and perhaps held another in her lap, would try to stay awake for the only time there was to read. She would feel again the weather of the outside on his cheek when, coming late from a meeting, he would find her so, and stimulated and ardent, sniffing her skin, coax: "I'll put the baby to bed, and you—put the book away, don't read, don't read."

That had been the most beguiling of all the "don't read, put your book away" her life had been. Chekhov indeed!

"Money?" She shrugged him off. "Could we get poorer than once we were? And in America, who starves?"

But as still he pressed:

"Let me alone about money. Was there ever enough? Seven little ones—for every penny I had to ask—and sometimes, remember, there was nothing. But always *I* had to manage. Now *you* manage. Rub your nose in it good."

But from those years she had had to manage, old humiliations and terrors rose up, lived again, and forced her to relive them. The children's needings; that grocer's face or this merchant's wife she had had to beg credit from when credit was a disgrace, the scenery of the long blocks walked around when she could not pay; school coming, and the desperate going over the old to see what could yet be remade; the soups of meat bones begged "for-the-dog" one winter. . . .

Enough. Now they had no children. Let *him* wrack his head for how they would live. She would not exchange her solitude for anything. *Never again to be forced to move to the rhythms of others.*   control vs. power

For in this solitude she had won to a reconciled peace.

Tranquility from having the empty house no longer an enemy, for it stayed clean—not as in the days when it was her family, the life in it, that had seemed the enemy: tracking, smudging, littering, dirtying, engaging her in endless defeating battle—and on whom her endless defeat had been spewed.

The few old books, memorized from rereading; the pictures to ponder (the magnifying glass superimposed on her heavy eyeglasses). Or if she wishes, when he is gone, the phonograph, that if she turns up very loud and strains, she can hear: the ordered sounds and the struggling.

Out in the garden, growing things to nurture. Birds to be kept out of the pear tree, and when the pears are heavy and ripe, the old fury of work, for all must be canned, nothing wasted.

And her one social duty (for she will not go to luncheons or meetings) the boxes of old clothes left with her, as with a life-practiced eye for finding what is still wearable within the worn (again the magnifying glass superimposed on the heavy glasses) she scans and sorts—this for rag or rummage, that for mending and cleaning, and this for sending abroad.

Being able at last to live within, and not move to the rhythms of others, as life had helped her to: denying; removing; isolating; taking the children one by one; then deafening, half-blinding—and at last, presenting her solitude.

And in it she had won to a reconciled peace.

Now he was violating it with his constant campaigning: *Sell the house and move to the Haven.* (You sit, you sit—there too you could sit like a stone.) He was making of her a battleground where old grievances tore. (Turn on your ear button—I'm talking.) And stubbornly she resisted—so that from wheedling, reasoning, manipulation, it was bitterness he now started with.

And it came to where every happening lashed up a quarrel.

"I will sell the house anyway," he flung at her one night. "I am putting it up for sale. There will be a way to make you sign."

The television blared, as always it did on the evenings he stayed home, and as always it reached her only as noise. She did not know if the tumult was in her or outside. Snap! she turned the sound off. "Shadows," she whispered to him, pointing to the screen, "look, it is only shadows." And in a scream: "Did you say that you will sell the house? Look at me, not at that. I am no shadow. You cannot sell without me."

"Leave on the television. I am watching."

"Like Paulie, like Jenny, a four-year-old. Staring at shadows. *You cannot sell the house.*"

"I will. We are going to the Haven. There you would not hear the television when you do not want it. I could sit in the social room and watch. You could lock yourself up to smell your unpleasantness in a room by yourself—for who would want to come near you?"

"No, no selling." A whisper now.

"The television is shadows. Mrs. Enlightened! Mrs.

Cultured! A world comes into your house—and it is shadows. People you would never meet in a thousand lifetimes. Wonders. When you were four years old, yes, like Paulie, like Jenny, did you know of Indian dances, alligators, how they use bamboo in Malaya? No, you scratched in your dirt with the chickens and thought Olshana was the world. Yes, Mrs. Unpleasant, I will sell the house, for there better can we be rid of each other than here."

She did not know if the tumult was outside, or in her. Always a ravening inside, a pull to the bed, to lie down, to succumb.

"Have you thought maybe Ma should let a doctor have a look at her?" asked their son Paul after Sunday dinner, regarding his mother crumpled on the couch, instead of, as was her custom, busying herself in Nancy's kitchen.

"Why not the President too?"

"Seriously, Dad. This is the third Sunday she's lain down like that after dinner. Is she that way at home?"

"A regular love affair with the bed. Every time I start to talk to her."

Good protective reaction, observed Nancy to herself. The workings of hos-til-ity.

"Nancy could take her. I just don't like how she looks. Let's have Nancy arrange an appointment."

"You think she'll go?" regarding his wife gloomily. "All right, we have to have doctor bills, we have to have doctor bills." Loudly: "Something hurts you?"

She startled, looked to his lips. He repeated: "Mrs. Take It Easy, something hurts?"

"Nothing. . . . Only you."

"A woman of honey. That's why you're lying down?"

"Soon I'll get up to do the dishes, Nancy."

"Leave them, Mother, I like it better this way."

"Mrs. Take It Easy, Paul says you should start ballet. You should go to see a doctor and ask: how soon can you start ballet?"

"A doctor?" she begged. "Ballet?"

"We were talking, Ma," explained Paul, "you don't seem any too well. It would be a good idea for you to see a doctor for a checkup."

"I get up now to do the kitchen. Doctors are bills and foolishness, my son. I need no doctors."

"At the Haven," he could not resist pointing out, "a doctor is *not* bills. He lives beside you. You start to sneeze, he is there before you open up a Kleenex. You can be sick there for free, all you want."

"Diarrhoea of the mouth, is there a doctor to make you dumb?"

"Ma. Promise me you'll go. Nancy will arrange it."

"It's all of a piece when you think of it," said Nancy, "the way she attacks my kitchen, scrubbing under every cup hook, doing the inside of the oven so I can't enjoy Sunday dinner, knowing that half-blind or not, she's going to find every speck of dirt. . . ."

"Don't, Nancy, I've told you—it's the only way she knows to be useful. What did the *doctor* say?"

"A real fatherly lecture. Sixty-nine is young these days. Go out, enjoy life, find interests. Get a new hearing aid, this one is antiquated. Old age is sickness only if one makes it so. Geriatrics, Inc."

"So there was nothing physical."

"Of course there was. How can you live to yourself like she does without there being? Evidence of a kidney disorder, and her blood count is low. He gave her a diet, and she's to come back for a follow-up and lab work. . . . But he was clear enough: Number One prescription—start living like a human being. When I think of your dad, who can really play the invalid with that arthritis of his as active as a teenager, and twice as much fun. . . ."

"You didn't tell me the doctor says your sickness is in you, how you live." He pushed his advantage. "Life and enjoyments you need better than medicine. And this diet, how can you keep it? To weigh each morsel and scrape away the bits of fat to make this soup, that pudding. There, at the Haven, they have a dietician, they would do it for you."

She is silent.

"You would feel better there, I know it," he says gently. "There there is life and enjoyments all around."

"What is the matter, Mr. Importantbusy, you have no card game or meeting you can go to?"—turning her face to the pillow.

For a while he cut his meetings and going out, fussed over her diet, tried to wheedle her into leaving the house, brought in visitors:

"I should come to a fashion tea. I should sit and look at pretty babies in clothes I cannot buy. This is pleasure?"

"Always you are better than everyone else. The doctor said you should go out. Mrs. Brem comes to you with goodness and you turn her away."

"Because *you* asked her to, she asked me."

"They won't come back. People you need, the doctor said. Your own cousins I asked; they were willing to come and make peace as if nothing had happened. . . ."

"No more crushers of people, pushers, hypocrites, around me. No more in *my* house. You go to them if you like."

"Kind he is to visit. And you, like ice."

"A babbler. All my life around babblers. Enough!"

"She's even worse, Dad? Then let her stew a while," advised Nancy. "You can't let it destroy you; it's a psychological thing, maybe too far gone for any of us to help."

So he let her stew. More and more she lay silent in bed, and sometimes did not even get up to make the meals. No longer was the tongue-lashing inevitable if he left the coffee cup where it did not belong, or forgot to take out the garbage or mislaid the broom. The birds grew bold that summer and for once pocked the pears, undisturbed.

A bellyful of bitterness and every day the same quarrel in a new way and a different old grievance the quarrel forced her to enter and relive. And the new torment: I am not really sick, the doctor said it, then why do I feel so sick?

One night she asked him: "You have a meeting tonight? Do not go. Stay . . . with me."

He had planned to watch "This Is Your Life" anyway, but half sick himself from the heavy heat, and sickening therefore the more after the brooks and woods of the Haven, with satisfaction he grated:

"Hah, Mrs. Live Alone And Like It wants company all of a sudden. It doesn't seem so good the time of solitary when she was a girl exile in Siberia. 'Do not go. Stay with me.' A new song for Mrs. Free As A Bird. Yes, I am going out, and while I am gone chew this aloneness good, and think how you keep us both from where if you want people you do not need to be alone."

"Go, go. All your life you have gone without me."

After him she sobbed curses he had not heard in years, old-country curses from their childhood: Grow, oh shall you grow like an onion, with your head in the ground. Like the hide of a drum shall you be, beaten in life, beaten in death. Oh shall you be like a chandelier, to hang, and to burn. . . .

She was not in their bed when he came back. She lay on the cot on the sun-porch. All week she did not speak or come near him; not did he try to make peace or care for her.

He slept badly, so used to her next to him. After all the years, old harmonies and dependencies deep in their bodies; she curled to him, or he coiled to her each warmed, warming, turning as the other turned, the nights a long embrace.

It was not the empty bed or the storm that woke him, but a faint singing. *She* was singing. Shaking off the drops of rain, the lightning riving her lifted face, he saw her so; the cot covers on the floor.

"This is a private concert?" he asked. "Come in, you are wet."

"I can breathe now," she answered; "my lungs are rich." Though indeed the sound was hardly a breath.

"Come in, come in." Loosing the bamboo shades.

"Look how wet you are." Half helping, half carrying her, still faint-breathing her song.

A Russian love song of fifty years ago.

He had found a buyer, but before he told her, he called together those children who were close enough to come. Paul, of course, Sammy from New Jersey, Hannah from Connecticut, Vivi from Ohio.

With a kindling of energy for her beloved visitors, she arrayed the house, cooked and baked. She was not prepared for the solemn after-dinner conclave, they too probing in and tearing. Her frightened eyes watched from mouth to mouth as each spoke.

His stories were eloquent and funny of her refusal to go back to the doctor; of the scorned invitations; of her stubborn silences or the bile "like a Niagara"; of her contrariness: "If I clean it's no good how I cleaned; if I don't clean, I'm still a master who thinks he has a slave."

("Vinegar he poured on me all his life; I am well marinated; how can I be honey now?")

Deftly he marched in the rightness for moving to the Haven; their money from social security free for visiting the children, not sucked into daily needs and into the house; the activities in the Haven for him; but mostly the Haven for *her*: her health, her need of care, distraction, amusement, friends who shared her interests.

"This does offer an outlet for Dad," said Paul; "he's always been an active person. And economic peace of mind isn't to be sneezed at, either. I could use a little of that myself."

But when they asked: "And you, Ma, how do you feel about it?" could only whisper:

"For him it is good. It is not for me. I can no longer live between people."

"You lived all your life *for* people," Vivi cried.

"Not with." Suffering doubly for the unhappiness on her children's faces.

"You have to find some compromise," Sammy insisted. "Maybe sell the house and buy a trailer. After forty-seven years there's surely some way you can find to live in peace."

"There is no help, my children. Different things we need."

"Then live alone!" He could control himself no longer. "I have a buyer for the house. Half the money for you, half for me. Either alone or with me to the Haven. You think I can live any longer as we are doing now?"

"Ma doesn't have to make a decision this minute, however you feel, Dad," Paul said quickly, "and you wouldn't want her to. Let's let it lay a few months, and then talk some more."

"I think I can work it out to take Mother home with me for a while," Hannah said. "You both look terrible, but especially you, Mother. I'm going to ask Phil to have a look at you."

"Sure," cracked Sammy. "What's the use of a doctor husband if you can't get free service out of him once in a while for the family? And absence might make the heart . . . you know."

"There was something after all," Paul told Nancy in a colorless voice. "That was Hannah's Phil calling. Her gall bladder. . . . Surgery."

"Her *gall* bladder. If that isn't classic. 'Bitter as gall'—talk of psychosom—"

He stepped closer, put his hand over her mouth and said in the same colorless, plodding voice. "We have to get Dad. They operated at once. The cancer was everywhere, surrounding the liver, everywhere. They did what they could . . . at best she has a year. Dad . . . we have to tell him."

2

Honest in his weakness when they told him, and that she was not to know. "I'm not an actor. She'll know right away by how I am. Oh that poor woman. I am old too, it will break me into pieces. Oh that poor woman. She will spit on me: 'So my sickness was how I live.' Oh Paulie, how she will be, that poor woman. Only she should not suffer. . . . I can't stand sickness, Paulie, I can't go with you."

But went. And play-acted.

"A grand opening and you did not even wait for me. . . . A good thing Hannah took you with her."

"Fashion teas I needed. They cut out what tore in me; just in my throat something hurts yet. . . . Look! So many flowers, like a funeral. Vivi called, did Hannah tell you? And Lennie from San Francisco, and Clara; and Sammy's coming." Her gnome's face pressed happily into the flowers.

It is impossible to predict in these cases, but once over the immediate effects of the operation, she should have several months of comparative well-being.

The money, where will come the money?

Travel with her, Dad. Don't take her home to the old associations. The other children will want to see her.

The money, where will I wring the money?

Whatever happens, she is not to know. No, you can't ask her to sign papers to sell the house; nothing to upset her. Borrow instead, then after. . . .

I had wanted to leave you each a few dollars to make life easier, as other fathers do. There will be nothing left now. (Failure! you and your "business is exploitation." Why didn't you make it when it could be made—Is that what you're thinking, Sammy?)

Sure she's unreasonable, Dad—but you have to stay with her; if there's to be any happiness in what's left of her life, it depends on you.

Prop me up, children. Think of me, too. Shuffled, chained with her, bitter woman. No Haven, and the little money going. . . . How happy she looks, poor creature.

The look of excitement. The straining to hear everything (the new hearing aid turned full). Why are you so happy, dying woman?

How the petals are, fold on fold, and the gladioli color. The autumn air.

Stranger grandsons, tall above the little gnome grandmother, the little spry grandfather. Paul in a frenzy of picture-taking before going.

She, wandering the great house. Feeling the books; laughing at the maple shoemaker's bench of a hundred years ago used as a table. The ear turned to music.

"Let us go home. See how good I walk now." "One step from the hospital," he answers, "and she wants to fly. Wait till Doctor Phil says."

"Look—the birds too are flying home. Very good Phil is and will not show it, but he is sick of sickness by the time he comes home."

"Mrs. Telepathy, to read minds," he answers; "read mine what it says: when the trunks of medicines become a suitcase, then we will go."

The grandboys, they do not know what to say to

us. . . . Hannah, she runs around here, there, when is there time for herself?

Let us go home. Let us go home.

Musing; gentleness—*but for the incidents of the rabbi in the hospital, and of the candles of benediction.*

Of the rabbi in the hospital:

Now tell me what happened, Mother.

From the sleep I awoke, Hannah's Phil, and he stands there like a devil in a dream and calls me by name. I cannot hear. I think he prays. Go away, please, I tell him, I am not a believer. Still he stands, while my heart knocks with fright.

You scared *him*, Mother. He thought you were delirious.

Who sent him? Why did he come to me?

It is a custom. The men of God come to visit those of their religion they might help. The hospital makes up the list for them—race, religion—and you are on the Jewish list.

Not for rabbis. At once go and make them change. Tell them to write: Race, human; Religion, none.

And of the candles of benediction:

Look how you have upset yourself, Mrs. Excited Over Nothing. Pleasant memories you should leave. Go in, go back to Hannah and the lights. Two weeks I saw candles and said nothing. But she asked me.

So what is so terrible? She forgets you never did, she asks you to light the Friday candles and say the benediction like Phil's mother when she visits. If the candles give her pleasure, why shouldn't she have the pleasure?

Not for pleasure she does it. For emptiness. Because his family does. Because all around her do.

That is not a good reason too? But you did not hear her. For heritage, she told you. For the boys, from the past they should have tradition.

Superstition! From the savages, afraid of the dark, of themselves: mumbo words and magic lights to scare away ghosts.

She told you: how it started does not take away the goodness. For centuries, peace in the house it means.

Swindler! Does she look back on the dark centuries? Candles bought instead of bread and stuck into a potato for a candlestick? Religion that stifled and said: in Paradise, woman, you will be the footstool of your husband, and in life—poor chosen Jew—ground under, despised, trembling in cellars. And cremated. And cremated.

This is religion's fault? You think you are still an orator of the 1905 revolution? Where are the pills for quieting? Which are they?

Heritage. How have we come from the savages, how no longer to be savages—this to teach. To look back and learn what ennobles man—this to teach.

To smash all ghettos that divide man—not to go back, not to go back—this to teach. Learned books in the house, will man live or die, and she gives to her boys—superstition.

Hannah that is so good to you. Take your pill, Mrs. Excited For Nothing, swallow.

Heritage! But when did I have time to teach? Of Hannah I asked only hands to help.

Swallow.

Otherwise—musing; gentleness.

Not to travel. To go home.

The children want to see you. We have to show them you are as thorny a flower as ever.

Not to travel.

Vivi wants you should see her new baby. She sent the tickets—aeroplane tickets—a Mrs. Roosevelt she wants to make of you. To Vivi's we have to go.

Vivis house

A new baby. How many warm, seductive babies. She holds him stiffly, *away* from her, so that he wails. And a long shudder begins, and the sweat beads on her forehead.

"Hush, shush," croons the grandfather, lifting him back. "You should forgive your grandmamma, little prince, she has never held a baby before, only seen them in glass cases. Hush, shush."

"You're tired, Ma," says Vivi. "The travel and the noisy dinner. I'll take you to lie down."

(A long travel from, to, what the feel of a baby evokes.)

In the aeroplane, cunningly designed to encase from motion (no wind, no feel of flight), she had sat severely and still, her face turned to the sky through which they cleaved and left no scar.

So this was how it looked, the determining, the crucial sky, and this was how man moved through it, remote above the dwindled earth, the concealed human life. Vulnerable life, that could scar.

There was a steerage ship of memory that shook across a great, circular sea: clustered, ill human beings; and through the thick-stained air, tiny fretting waters in a window round like the aeroplane's—sun round, moon round. (The round thatched roofs of Olshana.) Eye round—like the smaller window that framed distance the solitary year of exile when only her eyes could travel, and no voice spoke. And the polar winds hurled themselves across snow trackless and endless and white—like the clouds which had closed together below and hidden the earth.

Now they put a baby in her lap. Do not ask me, she would have liked to beg. Enough the worn face of Vivi, the remembered grandchildren. I cannot, cannot. . . .

Cannot what? Unnatural grandmother, not able to make herself embrace a baby.

She lay there in the bed of the two little girls, her new hearing aid turned full, listening to the sound of the children going to sleep, the baby's fretful crying and hushing, the clatter of dishes being washed and put away. They thought she slept. Still she rode on.

It was not that she had not loved her babies, her children. The love—the passion of tending—had risen with the need like a torrent; and like a torrent drowned and immolated all else. But when the need was done—oh the power that was lost in the painful damming back and drying up of what still surged, but had nowhere to go. Only the thin pulsing left that could not quiet, suffering over lives one felt, but could no longer hold nor help.

On that torrent she had borne them to their own lives, and the river-bed was desert long years now. Not there would she dwell, a memoried wraith. Surely that was not all, surely there was more. Still the springs, the springs were in her seeking. Somewhere an older power that beat for life. Somewhere coherence, transport, meaning. If they would but leave her in the air now stilled of clamour, in the reconciled solitude, to journey to her self.

And they put a baby in her lap. Immediacy to embrace, and the breath of *that* past: warm flesh like this that had claims and nuzzled away all else and with lovely mouths devoured; hot-living like an animal—intensely and now; the turning maze; the long drunkenness; the drowning into needing and being needed. Severely she looked back—and the shudder seized her again, and the sweat. Not that way. Not there, not now could she, not yet. . . .

And all that visit, she could not touch the baby.

"Daddy, is it the . . . sickness she's like that?" asked Vivi. "I was so glad to be having the baby—for her. I told Tim, it'll

126

give her more happiness than anything, being around a baby again. And she hasn't played with him once."

He was not listening, "Aahh little seed of life, little charmer," he crooned, "Hollywood should see you. A heart of ice you would melt. Kick, kick. The future you'll have for a ball. In 2050 still kick. Kick for your grandaddy then."

Attentive with the older children; sat through their performances (command performance; we command you to be the audience); helped Ann sort autumn leaves to find the best for a school programme; listened gravely to Richard tell about his rock collection, while her lips mutely formed the words to remember: *igneous, sedimentary, metamorphic;* looked for missing socks, books and bus tickets; watched the children whoop after their grandfather who knew how to tickle, chuck, lift, toss, do tricks, tell secrets, make jokes, match riddle for riddle. (Tell me a riddle, Grammy. I know no riddles, child.) Scrubbed sills and woodwork and furniture in every room; folded the laundry; straightened drawers; emptied the heaped baskets waiting for ironing (while he or Vivi or Tim nagged: You're supposed to rest here, you've been sick) but to none tended or gave food—and could not touch the baby.

After a week she said: "Let us go home. Today call about the tickets."

"You have important business, Mrs. Inahurry? The President waits to consult with you?" He shouted, for the fear of the future raced in him. "The clothes are still warm from the suitcase, your children cannot show enough how glad they are to see you, and you want home. There is plenty of time for home. We cannot be with the children at home."

"Blind to around you as always: the little ones sleep four in a room because we take their bed. We are two more people in a house with a new baby, and no help."

"Vivi is happy so. The children should have their grand-parents a while, she told to me. I should have my mommy and daddy. . . ."

"Babbler and blind. Do you look at her so tired? How she starts to talk and she cries? I am not strong enough yet to help. Let us go home."

(To reconciled solitude.)

For it seemed to her the crowded noisy house was listening to her, listening for her. She could feel it like a great ear pressed under her heart. And everything knocked: quick constant raps; let me in, let me in.

How was it that soft reaching tendrils also became blows that knocked?

C'mon, Grandma, I want to show you. . . .

Tell me a riddle, Grandma. *(I know no riddles)*

Look, Grammy, he's so dumb he can't even find his hands. (Dody and the baby on a blanket over the fermenting autumn mound)

I made them—for you. (Flat paper dolls with aprons that lifted on scalloped skirts that lifted on flowered pants; hair of yarn and great ringed questioning eyes) (Ann)

Watch me, Grandma. (Richard snaking up the tree,

hanging exultant, free, with one hand at the top. Below Dody hunching over in pretend-cooking.)

(Climb too, Dody, climb and look)

Be my nap bed, Grammy. (The "No!" too late.)

Morty's abandoned heaviness, while his fingers ladder up and down her hearing-aid cord to his drowsy chant: eentsiebeentsiespider. *(Children trust.)*

It's to start off your own rock collection, Grandma. That's a trilobite fossil, 200 million years old (millions of years on a boy's mouth) and that one's obsidian, black glass.

Knocked and knocked.

Mother, I *told* you the teacher said we had to bring it back all filled out this morning. Didn't you even ask Daddy? Then tell *me* which plan and I'll check it: evacuate or stay in the city or wait for you to come and take me away. (Seeing the look of straining to hear.) It's for Disaster, Grandma. *(Children trust)*

Vivi in the maze of the long, the lovely drunkenness.

The old old noises: baby sounds; screaming of a mother flayed to exasperation; children quarrelling; children playing; singing; laughter.

And Vivi's tears and memories, spilling so fast, half the words not understood.

She had started remembering out loud deliberately, so her mother would know the past was cherished, still lived in her.

Nursing the baby: My friends marvel, and I tell them,

oh it's easy to be such a cow. I remember how beautiful my mother seemed nursing my brother, and the milk just flows . . . . Was that Davy? It must have been Davy. . . .

Past view

Lowering a hem: How did you ever . . . when I think how you made everything we wore . . . Tim, just think, seven kids and Mommy sewed everything . . . do I remember you sang while you sewed? That white dress with the red apples on the skirt you fixed over for me, was it Hannah's or Clara's before it was mine?

Washing sweaters: Ma, I'll never forget, one of those days so nice you washed clothes outside; one of the first spring days it must have been. The bubbles just danced up and down while you scrubbed, and we chased after, and you stopped to show us how to blow our own bubbles with green onion stalks . . . you always. . . .

"Strong onion, to still make you cry after so many years," her father said, to turn the tears into laughter.

While Richard bent over his homework: Where is it now, do we still have it, the Book of the Martyrs? It always seemed so, well—exalted, when you'd put it on the round table and we'd all look at it together; there was even a halo from the lamp. The lamp with the beaded fringe you could move up and down; they're in style again, pulley lamps like that, but without the fringe. You know the book I'm talking about, Daddy, the Book of the Martyrs, the first picture was a bust of Socrates? I wish there was something like that for the children, Mommy, to give them what you. . . . (And the tears splashed again)

(What I intended and did not? Stop it, daughter, stop it, leave that time. And he, the hypocrite, sitting there with tears in his eyes—it was nothing to you then, nothing.)

. . . The time you came to school and I almost died of shame because of your accent and because I knew you knew I was ashamed; how could I? . . . Sammy's harmonica and you danced to it once, yes you did, you and Davy squealing in your arms. . . . That time you bundled us up and walked us down to the railway station to stay the night 'cause it was heated and we didn't have any coal, that winter of the strike, you didn't think I remembered that, did you, Mommy? . . . How you'd call us out to see the sunsets. . . .

Day after day, the spilling memories. Worse now, questions, too. Even the grandchildren: Grandma, in the olden days, when you were little. . . .

It was the afternoons that saved.

While they thought she napped, she would leave the mosaic on the wall (of children's drawings, maps, calendars, pictures, Ann's cardboard dolls with their great ringed questioning eyes) and hunch in the girls' cupboard, on the low shelf where the shoes stood, and the girls' dresses covered.

For that while she would painfully sheathe against the listening house, the tendrils and noises that knocked, and Vivi's spilling memories. Sometimes it helped to braid and unbraid the sashes that dangled, or to trace the pattern on the hoop slips.

Today she had jacks and children under jet trails to

forget. Last night, Ann and Dody silhouetted in the window against a sunset of flaming man-made clouds of jet trail, their jacks ball accenting the peaceful noise of dinner being made. Had she told them, yes she had told them of how they played jacks in her village though there was no ball, no jacks. Six stones, round and flat, toss them out, the seventh on the back of the hand, toss, catch and swoop as many as possible, toss again. . . .

Of stones (repeating Richard) there are three kinds: earth's fire jetting; rock of layered centuries; crucibled new out of the old *(igneous, sedimentary, metamorphic)*. But there was that other—frozen to black glass, never to transform or hold the fossil memory . . . (let not my seed fall on stone). There was an ancient man who fought to heights a great rock that crashed back down eternally—eternal labour, freedom, labour . . . (stone will perish, but the word remain). And you, David, who with a stone slew, screaming: Lord, take my heart of stone and give me flesh.

Who was screaming? Why was she back in the common room of the prison, the sun motes dancing in the shafts of light, and the informer being brought in, a prisoner now, like themselves. And Lisa leaping, yes, Lisa, the gentle and tender, biting at the betrayer's jugular. Screaming and screaming.

No, it is the children screaming. Another of Paul and Sammy's terrible fights?

In Vivi's house. Severely: you are in Vivi's house.

Blows, screams, a call: "Grandma!" For her? Oh please not for her. Hide, hunch behind the dresses deeper. But a trembling little body hurls itself beside her—surprised, smothered laughter, arms surround her neck, tears rub dry on her cheek, and words too soft to understand whisper into her ear (Is this where you hide too, Grammy? It's my secret place, we have a secret now).

And the sweat beads, and the long shudder seizes.

It seemed the great ear pressed inside now, and the knocking. "We have to go home," she told him, "I grow ill here."

"It is your own fault, Mrs. Bodybusy, you do not rest, you do too much." He raged, but the fear was in his eyes. "It was a serious operation, they told you to take care. . . . All right, we will go to where you can rest."

But where? Not home to death, not yet. He had thought to Lennie's, to Clara's; beautiful visits with each of the children. She would have to rest first, be stronger. If they could but go to Florida—it glittered before him, the never-realized promise of Florida. California: of course. (The money, the money, dwindling!) Los Angeles first for sun and rest, then to Lennie's in San Francisco.

He told her the next day. "You saw what Nancy wrote: snow and wind back home, a terrible winter. And look at you—all bones and a swollen belly. I called Phil: he said: 'A prescription, Los Angeles sun and rest.'"

She watched the words on his lips. "You have sold the house," she cried, "that is why we do not go home. That is why you talk no more of the Haven. Why there is money for travel. After the children you will drag me to the Haven."

"The Haven! Who thinks of the Haven any more? Tell her, Vivi, tell Mrs. Suspicious: a prescription, sun and rest, to make you healthy. . . . And how could I sell the house without *you*?"

At the place of farewells and greetings, of winds of coming and winds of going, they say their good-byes.

They look back at her with the eyes of others before them: Richard with her own blue blaze; Ann with the Nordic eyes of Tim; Morty's dreaming brown of a great-grandmother he will never know; Dody with the laughing eyes of him who had been her springtide love (who stands beside her now); Vivi's, all tears.

The baby's eyes are closed in sleep.

Good-bye, my children.

3

It is to the back of the great city he brought her, to the dwelling places of the cast-off old. Bounded by two lines of amusement piers to the north and to the south, and between a long straight paving rimmed with black benches facing the sand—sands so wide the ocean is only a far fluting.

In the brief vacation season, some of the boarded stores fronting the sands open, and families, young people and children, may be seen. A little tasselled tram shuttles between the piers, and the lights of roller coasters prink and tweak over those who come to have sensation made in them.

The rest of the year it is abandoned to the old, all else

boarded up and still; seemingly empty, except the occasional days and hours when the sun, like a tide, sucks them out of the low rooming houses, casts them on to the benches and sandy rim of the walk—and sweeps them into decaying enclosures back again.

A few newer apartments glint among the low bleached squares. It is in one of these Lennie's Jeannie has arranged their rooms. "Only a few miles north and south people pay hundreds of dollars a month for just this gorgeous air, Grandaddy, just this ocean closeness."

She had been ill on the plane, lay ill for days in the unfamiliar room. Several times the doctor came by—left medicine she would not take. Several times Jeannie drove in the twenty miles from work, still in her Visiting Nurse uniform, the lightness and brightness of her like a healing.

"Who can believe it is winter?" he asked one morning. "Beautiful it is outside like an ad. Come, Mrs. Invalid, come to taste it. You are well enough to sit in here, you are well enough to sit outside. The doctor said it too."

But the benches were encrusted with people, and the sands at the sidewalk's edge. Besides, she had seen the far ruffle of the sea: "there take me," and though she leaned against him, it was she who led.

Plodding and plodding, sitting often to rest, he grumbling. Patting the sand so warm. Once she scooped up a handful, cradling it close to her better eye; peered, and flung it back. And as they came almost to the brink and she could see the glistening wet, she sat down, pulled off her shoes and stockings, left him and began to run. "You'll catch cold," he screamed, but the sand in his shoes weighed him down—he who had always been the agile one—and already the white spray creamed her feet.

He pulled her back, took a handkerchief to wipe off the wet and the sand. "Oh no," she said, "the sun will dry," seized the square and smoothed it flat, dropped on it a mound of sand, knotted the kerchief corners and tied it to a bag—"to look at with the strong glass" (for the first time in years explaining an action of hers)—and lay down with the little bag against her cheek, looking toward the shore that nurtured life as it first crawled toward consciousness the millions of years ago.

He took her one Sunday in the evil-smelling bus, past flat miles of blister houses, to the home of relatives. Oh what is this? She cried as the light began to smoke and the houses to dim and recede. Smog, he said, everyone knows but you . . . . Outside he kept his arms about her, but she walked with hands pushing the heavy air as if to open it, whispered: who has done this? Sat down suddenly to vomit at the curb and for a long while refused to rise.

One's age as seen on the altered face of those known in youth. Is this they he has come to visit? This Max and Rose, smooth and pleasant, introducing them to polite children, disinterested grandchildren, "the whole family, once a month on Sundays. And why not? We have the room, the help, the food."

Talk of cars, of houses, of success: this son that, that

daughter this. And *your* children? Hastily skimped over, the intermarriages, the obscure work—"my doctor son-in-law, Phil"—all he has to offer. She silent in a corner. (Car-sick like a baby, he explains.) Years since he has taken her to visit anyone but the children, and old apprehensions prickle: "no incidents," he silently begs, "no incidents." He itched to tell them. "A very sick woman," significantly, indicating her with his eyes, "a very sick woman." Their restricted faces did not react. "Have you thought maybe she'd do better at Palm Springs?" Rose asked. "Or at least a nicer section of the beach, nicer people, a pool." Not to have to say "money" he said instead: "would she have sand to look at through a magnifying glass?" and went on, detail after detail, the old habit betraying of parading the queerness of her for laughter.

After dinner—the others into the living-room in men- or women-clusters, or into the den to watch TV—the four of them alone. She sat close to him, and did not speak. Jokes, stories, people they had known, beginning of reminiscence, Russia fifty-sixty years ago. Strange words across the Duncan Phyfe table: *hunger; secret meetings; human rights; spies; betrayals; prison; escape*—interrupted by one of the grandchildren: "Commercial's on; any Coke left? Gee, you're missing a real hair-raiser." And then a granddaughter (Max proudly: "look at her, an American queen") drove them home on her way back to U.C.L.A. No incident—except that there had been no incidents.

The first few mornings she had taken with her the magnifying glass, but he would sit only on the benches, so she rested at the foot, where slatted bench shadows fell, and unless she turned her hearing aid down, other voices invaded.

Now on the days when the sun shone and she felt well enough, he took her on the tram to where the benches ranged in oblongs, some with tables for draughts or cards. Again the blanket on the sand in the striped shadows, but she no longer brought the magnifying glass. He played cards, and she lay in the sun and looked towards the waters; or they walked—two blocks down to the scaling hotel, two blocks back—past chili-hamburger stands, open-doored bars. Next to New and Perpetual Rummage Sale stores.

Once, out of the aimless walkers, slow and shuffling like themselves, someone ran unevenly towards them, embraced, kissed, wept: "dear friends, old friends." A friend of *hers*, not his: Mrs. Mays who had lived next door to them in Denver when the children were small.

Thirty years are compressed into a dozen sentences; and the present, not even in three. All is told: the children scattered; the husband dead; she lives in a room two blocks up from the sing hall—and points to the domed auditorium jutting before the pier. The leg? phlebitis; the heavy breathing? that, one does not ask. She, too, comes to the benches each day to sit. And tomorrow, tomorrow, are they going to the community sing? Of course he would have heard of it, everybody goes—the big doings they wait for all week.

They have never been? She will come for them to dinner tomorrow and they will all go together.

So it is that she sits in the wind of the singing, among the thousand various faces of age.

She had turned off her hearing aid at once they came into the auditorium—as she would have wished to turn off sight.

One by one they streamed by and imprinted on her—and though the savage zest of their singing came voicelessly soft and distant, the faces still roared—the faces densened the air—chorded into.

children-chants, mother-croons, singing of the
     chained;
love serenades, Beethoven storms, mad Lucia's
     scream;
drunken joy-songs, keens for the dead, work-singing

> *while from floor to balcony to dome a bare-footed sore-covered little girl threaded the sound-thronged tumult, danced her ecstasy of grimace to flutes that scratched at a cross-roads village wedding*

Yes, faces became sound, and the sound became faces; and faces and sound became weight—pushed, pressed

"Air"—her hand claws his.

"Whenever I enjoy myself. . . ." Then he saw the grey sweat on her face. "Here. Up. Help me, Mrs. Mays," and they support her out to where she can gulp the air in sob after sob.

"A doctor, we should get for her a doctor."

"Tch, it's nothing," says Ellen Mays, "I get it all the time. You've missed the tram; come to my place. Fix your hearing aid, honey . . . close . . . tea. My view. See, she *wants* to come. Steady now, that's how." Adding mysteriously: "Remember your advice, easy to keep your head above water, empty things float. Float."

The singing a fading march for them, tall woman with a swollen leg, weaving little man, and the swollen thinness they help between.

The stench in the hall: mildew? decay? "We sit and rest then climb. My gorgeous view. We help each other and here   we   are."

The stench along into the slab of room. A washstand for a sink, a box with oilcloth tacked around for a cupboard, a three-burner gas plate. Artificial flowers, colorless with dust. Everywhere pictures foaming: wedding, baby, party, vacation, graduation, family pictures. From the narrow couch under a slit of window, sure enough the view: lurching rooftops and a scallop of ocean heaving, preening, twitching under the moon.

"While the water heats. Excuse me . . . down the hall." Ellen Mays has gone.

"You'll live?" he asks mechanically, sat down to feel his fright; tried to pull her alongside.

She pushed him away. "For air," she said; stood clinging to the dresser. Then, in a terrible voice:

After a lifetime of room. Of many rooms.

Shhh.

You remember how she lived. Eight children. And now one room   like a coffin.

She pays rent!

Shrinking the life of her   into one room like a coffin Rooms and rooms like this. I lie on the quilt and hear them talk Once you went for coffee   I walked   I saw

Please, Mrs. Orator Without Breath.

A Balzac   a Chekhov to write it   Rummage Alone On scraps

Better here old than in the old country!

On scraps   And they sang like . . . like. . . . Wondrous. *Man, one has to believe.*   So strong. For what? To rot   not grow?

Your poor lungs beg you. They sob between each word.

Singing. Unused   the life   in them. She   in this poor room   with her   pictures.   Max   You   The   children everywhere   unused   the life   And who has meaning? Century after century   still all   in man not   to grow?

Coffins, rummage, plants: sick woman. Oh lay down. We will get for you the doctor.

"And when will it end. Oh, *the end.*" *That* nightmare thought, and this time she writhed, crumpled beside him, seized his hand (for a moment again the weight, the soft distant roaring of humanity) and on the strangled-for breath, begged: "Man . . . will destroy ourselves?"

And looking for answer—in the helpless pity and fear

for her (for *her*) that distorted his face—she understood the
last months, and knew that she was dying.

4

"Let us go home," she said after several days.

"You are in training for a cross-country trip? That is
why you do not even walk across the room? Here, like a
prescription Phil said, till you are stronger from the operation. You want to break doctor's orders?"

She saw the fiction was necessary to him, was silent;
then: "At home I will get better. If the doctor here says?"

"And winter? And the visits to Lennie and to Clara? All
right," for he saw the tears in her eyes, "I will write Phil, and
talk to the doctor."

Days passed. He reported nothing. Jeannie came and took
her out for air, past the boarded concessions, the hooded and
tented amusement rides, to the end of the pier. They watched
the spent waves feeding the new, the gulls in the clouded sky;
even up where they sat, the wind-blown sand stung.

She did not ask to go down the crooked steps to the sea.

Back in her bed, while he was gone to the store, she
said: "Jeannie, this doctor, he is not one I can ask questions.
Ask him for me, can I go home?"

Jeannie looked at her, said quickly: "Of course, poor
Granny. You want your own things around you, don't you?
I'll call him tonight. . . . Look, I've something to show you,"
and from her purse unwrapped a large cookie, intricately
shaped like a little girl.

"Look at the curls—can you hear me well, Granny?— and the darling eyelashes. I just came from a house where they were baking them."

"The dimples," she marvelled, "there in the knees," holding it to the better light, turning, studying, "like art. Each singly they cut, or a mould?"

"Singly," said Jeannie, "and if it is a child only the mother can make them. Oh Granny, it's the likeness of a real little girl who died yesterday—Rosita. She was three years old. *Pan del Muerto*, the Bread of the Dead. It was the custom in the part of Mexico they came from."

Still she turned and inspected. "Look, the hollow in the throat, the little cross necklace. . . . I think for the mother it is a good thing to be busy with such bread. You know the family?"

Jeannie nodded. "On my rounds. I nursed. . . . Oh Granny, it is like a party; they play songs she liked to dance to. The coffin is lined with pink velvet and she wears a white dress. There are candles. . . ."

"In the house?" Surprised, "They keep her in the house?"

"Yes," said Jeannie, "and it is against the health law. I think she is . . . prepared there. The father said it will be sad to bury her in this country; in Oaxaca they have a feast night with candles each year; everyone picnics on the graves of those they loved until dawn."

"Yes, Jeannie, the living must comfort themselves." And closed her eyes.

"You want to sleep, Granny?"

"Yes, tired from the pleasure of you. I may keep the Rosita? There stand it, on the dresser, where I can see; something of my own around me."

In the kitchenette, helping her grandfather unpack the groceries, Jeannie said in her light voice:

"I'm resigning my job, Grandaddy."

"Ah, the lucky young man. Which one is he?"

"Too late. You're spoken for." She made a pyramid of cans, unstacked, and built again.

"Something is wrong with the job?"

"With me. I can't be"—she searched for the word— "What they call professional enough. I let myself feel things. And tomorrow I have to report a family. . . ." The cans clicked again. "It's not that, either. I just don't know what I want to do, maybe go back to school, maybe go to art school. I thought if you went to San Francisco I'd come along and talk it over with Mommy and Daddy. But I don't see how you can go. She wants to go home. She asked me to ask the doctor."

The doctor told her himself. "Next week you may travel, when you are a little stronger." But next week there was the fever of an infection, and by the time that was over, she could not leave the bed—a rented hospital bed that stood beside the double bed he slept in alone now.

Outwardly the days repeated themselves. Every other afternoon and evening he went out to his newfound cronies, to talk and play cards. Twice a week, Mrs. Mays came. And the rest of the time, Jeannie was there.

By the sickbed stood Jeannie's FM radio. Often into the room the shapes of music came. She would lie curled on her side, her knees drawn up, intense in listening (Jeannie sketched her so, coiled, convoluted like an ear), then thresh her hand out and abruptly snap the radio mute—still to lie in her attitude of listening, concealing tears.

Once Jeannie brought in a young Marine to visit, a friend from high-school days she had found wandering near the empty pier. Because Jeannie asked him to, gravely, without self-consciousness, he sat himself cross-legged on the floor and performed for them a dance of his native Samoa.

Long after they left, a tiny thrumming sound could be heard where, in her bed, she strove to repeat the beckon, flight, surrender of his hands, the fluttering footbeats, and his low plaintive calls.

Hannah and Phil sent flowers. To deepen her pleasure, he placed one in her hair. "Like a girl," he said, and brought the hand mirror so she could see. She looked at the pulsing red flower, the yellow skull face; a desolate, excited laugh shuddered from her, and she pushed the mirror away—but let the flower burn.

The week Lennie and Helen came, the fever returned. With it the excited laugh, and incessant words. She, who in her life had spoken but seldom and then only when necessary (never having learned the easy, social uses of words), now in dying, spoke incessantly.

In a half-whisper: "Like Lisa she is, your Jeannie. Have I told you of Lisa, she who taught me to read? Of the highborn she was, but noble in herself. I was sixteen; they beat me; my father beat me so I would not go to her. It was forbidden, she was a Tolstoyan. At night, past dogs that howled, terrible dogs, my son, in the snows of winter to the road, I to ride in her carriage like a lady, to books. To her, life was holy, knowledge was holy, and she taught me to read. They hung her. Everything that happens one must try to understand why. She killed one who betrayed many. Because of betrayal, betrayed all she lived and believed. In one minute she killed, before my eyes (there is so much blood in a human being, my son), in prison with me. All that happens, one must try to understand.

"The name?" Her lips would work. "The name that was their pole star; the doors of the death houses fixed to open on it; I read of it my year of penal servitude. Thuban!" very excited, "Thuban, in ancient Egypt the pole star. Can you see, look out to see it, Jeannie, if it swings around *our* pole star that seems to *us* not to move.

"Yes, Jeannie, at your age my mother and grandmother had already buried children . . . yes, Jeannie, it is more than oceans between Olshana and you . . . yes, Jeannie, they danced, and for all the bodies they had they might as well be chickens, and indeed, they scratched and flapped their arms and hopped.

"And Andrei Yefimitch, who for twenty years had never known of it and never wanted to know, said as if he wanted to cry: but why my dear friend this malicious laughter?" telling to herself half-memorized phrases from her few books. "Pain I answer with tears and cries, baseness with indignation, meanness with repulsion . . . for life may be hated or wearied of, but never despised."

Delirious: "Tell me, my neighbor, Mrs. Mays, the pictures never lived, but what of the flowers? Tell them who ask: no rabbis, no ministers, no priests, no speeches, no ceremonies: ah, false—let the living comfort themselves. Tell Sammy's boy, he who flies, tell him to go to Stuttgart and see where Davy has no grave. And what?" A conspirator's laugh. "And what? where millions have no graves."

In delirium or not, wanting the radio on; not seeming to listen, the words still jetting, wanting the music on. Once, silencing it abruptly as of old, she began to cry, unconcealed tears this time. "You have pain, Granny?" Jeannie asked.

"The music," she said, "still it is there and we do not hear; knocks, and our poor human ears too weak. What else, what else we do not hear?"

Once she knocked his hand aside as he gave her a pill, swept the bottles from her bedside table: "no pills, let me feel what I feel," and laughed as on his hands and knees he groped to pick them up.

Night-times her hand reached across the bed to hold his.

A constant retching began. Her breath was too faint for sustained speech now, but still the lips moved:

When no longer necessary   to injure others

147

> *Pick   pick pick   Blind chicken*
> *As a human being   responsibility for*

"David!" imperious, "Basin!" and she would vomit, rinse her mouth, the wasted throat working to swallow, and begin the chant again.

She will be better off in the hospital now, the doctor said.

He sent the telegrams to the children, was packing her suitcase, when her hoarse voice startled. She had roused, was pulling herself to sitting.

"Where now?" she asked. "Where now do you drag me?"

"You do not even have to have a baby to go this time," he soothed, looking for the brush to pack. "Remember, after Davy you told me—worthy to have a baby for the pleasure of the hospital?"

"Where now? Not home yet?" Her voice mourned. "Where *is* my home?"

He rose to ease her back. "The doctor, the hospital," he started to explain, but deftly, like a snake, she had slithered out of bed and stood swaying, propped behind the night table.

"Coward," she hissed, "runner."

"You stand," he said senselessly.

"To take me there and run. Afraid of a little vomit."

He reached her as she fell. She struggled against him, half slipped from his arms, pulled herself up again.

"Weakling," she taunted, "to leave me there and run. Betrayer. All your life you have run."

He sobbed, telling Jeannie. "A Marilyn Monroe to run for her virtue. Fifty-nine pounds she weighs, the doctor said, and she beats at me like a Dempsey. Betrayer, she cries, and I running like a dog when she calls; day and night, running to her, her vomit, the bedpan. . . ."

"She wants you, Grandaddy," said Jeannie. "Isn't that what they call love? I'll see if she sleeps, and if she does, poor worn-out darling, we'll have a party, you and I; I brought us rum babas."

They did not move her. By her bed now stood the tall hooked pillar that held the solutions—blood and dextrose—to feed her veins. Jeannie moved down the hall to take over the sickroom, her face so radiant, her grandfather asked her once: "you are in love?" (Shameful the joy, the pure overwhelming joy from being with her grandmother; the peace, the serenity that breathed.) "My darling escape," she answered incoherently, "my darling Granny"—as if that explained.

Now one by one the children came, those that were able. Hannah, Paul, Sammy. Too late to ask: and what did you learn with your living, Mother, and what do we need to know?

Clara, the eldest, clenched:

> *Pay me back, Mother, pay me back for all you took from me. Those others you crowded into your heart. The hands I needed to be for you, the heaviness, the responsibility.*

> *Is this she? Noises the dying make, the crablike hands crawling over the covers. The ethereal singing.*

She hears that music, that singing from childhood; forgotten sound—not heard since, since. . . . And the hardness breaks like a cry: Where did we lose each other, first mother, singing mother?

Annulled: the quarrels, the gibing, the harshness between; the fall into silence and the withdrawal.

I do not know you, Mother. Mother, I never knew you.

Lennie, suffering not alone for her who was dying, but for that in her which never lived (for that which in him might never live). From him too, unspoken words: *good-bye Mother who taught me to mother myself.*

Not Vivi, who must stay with her children; not Davy, but he is already here, having to die again with *her* this time, for the living take their dead with them when they die.

Light she grew, like a bird, and, like a bird, sound bubbled in her throat while the body fluttered in agony. Night and day, asleep or awake (though indeed there was no difference now) the songs and the phrases leaping.

And he, who had once dreaded a long dying (from fear of himself, from horror of the dwindling money) now desired her quick death profoundly, for *her* sake. He no longer went out, except when Jeannie forced him; no longer laughed, except when, in the bright kitchenette, Jeannie coaxed his laughter (and she, who seemed to hear nothing else, would laugh too, conspiratorial wisps of laughter).

Light, like a bird, the fluttering body, the little claw hands, the beaked shadow on her face; and the throat, bubbling, straining.

He tried not to listen, as he tried not to look on the face in which only the forehead remained familiar, but trapped with her the long nights in that little room, the sounds worked themselves into his consciousness, with their punctuation of death swallows, whimpers, gurglings.

Even in reality (swallow) *life's lack of it*

The bell   Summon   what ennobles

78,000 in one minute (whisper of a scream) *78,000 human beings   destroy ourselves?*

"Aah, Mrs. Miserable," he said, as if she could hear, "all your life working, and now in bed you lie, servants to tend, you do not even need to call to be tended, and still you work. Such hard work it is to die? Such hard work?"

The body threshed, her hand clung in his. A melody, ghost-thin, hovered on her lips, and like a guilty ghost, the vision of her bent in listening to it, silencing the record instantly he was near. Now, heedless of his presence, she floated the melody on and on.

"Hid it from me," he complained, "how many times you listened to remember it so?" And tried to think when she had first played it, or first begun to silence her few records when he came near—but could reconstruct nothing. There was only this room with its tall hooked pillar and its swarm of sounds.

An unexamined life   not worth

Strong   with the not yet   in the now

Dogma dead   war dead   one country

"It helps, Mrs. Philosopher, words from books? It

helps?" And it seemed to him that for seventy years she had hidden a tape recorder, infinitely microscopic, within her, that it had coiled infinite mile on mile, trapping every song, every melody, every word read, heard and spoken—and that maliciously she was playing back only what said nothing of him, of the children, of their intimate life together.

"Left us indeed, Mrs. Babbler," he reproached, "you who called others babbler and cunningly saved your words. A lifetime you tended and loved, and now not a word of us, for us. Left us indeed? Left me."

And he took out his solitaire deck, shuffled the cards loudly, slapped them down.

Lift high   banner of reason   justice   freedom   light (tatter of an orator's voice)

Mankind   life worthy   heroic capacities

Seeks (blur of shudder) *belong   human being*

"Words, words," he accused, "and what human beings did *you* seek around you, Mrs. Live Alone, and what mankind think worthy?"

Though even as he spoke, he remembered she had not always been isolated, had not always wanted to be alone (as he knew there had been a voice before this gossamer one; before the hoarse voice that broke from silence to lash, make incidents, shame him—a girl's voice of eloquence that spoke their holiest dreams). But again he could reconstruct, image, nothing of what had been before, or when, or how, it had changed.

Ace, queen, jack. The pillar shadow fell, so, in two tracks;

in the mirror depths glistened a moonlike blob, the empty solution bottle. And it worked in him: *of reason and justice and free-*
dom. Dogma dead: he remembered the full quotation, laughed
bitterly. "Hah, good you do not know what you say; good
Victor Hugo died and did not see it, his twentieth century."

Deuce, ten, five. Dauntlessly she began a song of their
youth of belief:

> *These things shall be, a loftier race*
> *than e'er the world hath known shall rise*
> *with flame of freedom in their souls*
> *and light of knowledge in their eyes*

King, four jack. "In the twentieth century, hah!"

> *They shall be gentle, brave and strong*
> *to spill no drop of blood, but dare*
> *all that may plant man's lordship firm*
> *on earth and fire and sea and air*

"To spill no drop of blood, hah! So, cadaver, and you
too, cadaver Hugo, 'in the twentieth century ignorance will
be dead, dogma will be dead, war will be dead, and for all
mankind one country—of fulfillment.' Hah!"

> *And every life* (long strangling cough) *shall*
> *be a song*

The cards fell from his fingers. Without warning, the
bereavement and betrayal he had sheltered—compounded

through the years—hidden even from himself—revealed itself,

uncoiled,

released,

sprung

and with it the monstrous shapes of what had actually happened in the century.

A ravening hunger or thirst seized him. He groped into the kitchenette, switched on all three lights, piled a tray—"you have finished your night snack, Mrs. Cadaver, now I will have mine." And he was shocked at the tears that splashed on the tray.

"Salt tears. For free. I forgot to shake on salt?"

Whispered: "Lost, how much I lost."

Escaped to the grandchildren whose childhoods were childish, who had never hungered, who lived unravaged by disease in warm houses of many rooms, had all the school for which they cared, could walk on any street, stood a head taller than their grandparents, towered above—beautiful skins, straight backs, clear straightforward eyes. "Yes, you in Olshana," he said to the town of sixty years ago, "they would be nobility to you."

And was this not the dream then, come true in ways undreamed? he asked.

And are there no other children in the world? he answered, as if in her harsh voice.

And the flame of freedom, the light of knowledge?

And to spill no drop of blood?

And he thought that at six Jeannie would get up and

it would be his turn to go to her room and sleep, that he could press the buzzer and she would come now; that in the afternoon Ellen Mays was coming, and this time they would play cards and he could marvel at how rouge can stand half an inch on the cheek; that in the evening the doctor would come, and he could beg him to be merciful, to stop the feeding solutions, to let her die.

To let her die, and with her their youth of belief out of which her bright, betrayed words foamed; stained words, that on her working lips came stainless.

Hours yet before Jeannie's turn. He could press the buzzer and wake her to come now; he could take a pill, and with it sleep; he could pour more brandy into his milk glass, though what he had poured was not yet touched.

Instead he went back, checked her pulse, gently tended with his knotty fingers as Jeannie had taught.

She was whimpering; her hand crawled across the covers for his. Compassionately he enfolded it, and with his free hand gathered up the cards again. Still was there thirst or hunger ravening in him.

That world of their youth—dark, ignorant, terrible with hate and disease—how was it that living in it, in the midst of corruption, filth, treachery, degradation, they had not mistrusted man nor themselves; had believed so beautifully, so . . . falsely?

"Aaah, children," he said out loud, "how we believed, how we belonged." And he yearned to package for each of the children, the grandchildren, for everyone, *that joyous certainty, that sense of mattering, of moving and being moved, of being one and indivisible with the great of the past, with all that freed, ennobled man.* Package it, stand on corners, in front of stadiums and on crowded beaches knock on doors, give it as a fabled gift.

"And why not in cereal boxes, in soap packages?" he mocked himself. "Aah. You have taken my senses, cadaver."

Words foamed, died unsounded. Her body writhed; she made kissing motions with her mouth. (Her lips moving as she read, pouring over the Book of the Martyrs, the magnifying glass superimposed over the heavy eyeglasses.) *Still she believed?* "Eva!" he whispered. "Still you believed? You lived by it? These Things Shall Be?"

"One pound soup meat," she answered distinctly, "one soup bone."

"My ears heard you. Ellen Mays was witness: 'Man . . . one has to believe.'" Imploringly: "Eva!"

"Bread, day-old." She was mumbling. "Please, in a wooden box . . . for kindling. The thread, hah, the thread breaks. Cheap thread"—and a gurgling, enormously loud, began in her throat.

"I ask for stone; she gives me bread—day-old." He pulled his hand away, shouted: "Who wanted questions? Everything you have to wake?" Then dully, "Ah, let me help you turn, poor creature."

Words jumbled, cleared. In a voice of crowded terror:

"Paul, Sammy, don't fight.

"Hannah, have I ten hands?

156

"How can I give it, Clara, how can I give it if I don't have?"

"You lie," he said sturdily, "there was joy too." Bitterly: "Ah how cheap you speak of us at the last."

As if to rebuke him, as if her voice had no relationship with her flailing body, she sang clearly, beautifully, a school song the children had taught her when they were little; begged:

"Not look my hair where they cut. . . ."

(The crown of braids shorn.) And instantly he left the mute old woman pouring over the Book of the Martyrs; went past the mother treadling at the sewing machine, singing with the children; past the girl in her wrinkled prison dress, hiding her hair with scarred hands, lifting to him her awkward, shamed, imploring eyes of love; and took her in his arms, dear, personal, fleshed, in all the heavy passion he had loved to rouse from her.

"Eva!"

Her little claw hand beat the covers. How much, how much can a man stand? He took up the cards, put them down, circled the beds, walked to the dresser, opened, shut drawers, brushed his hair, moved his hand bit by bit over the mirror to see what of the reflection he could blot out with each move, and felt that at any moment he would die of what was unendurable. Went to press the buzzer to wake Jeannie, looked down, saw on Jeannie's sketch pad the hospital bed, with *her*; the double bed alongside, with him; the tall pillar feeding into her veins, and their hands, his and hers, clasped, feeding each other. And as if he had been instructed he went to his bed, lay down, holding the sketch as if it could shield against the monstrous shapes of loss, of betrayal, of death—and with his free hand took hers back into his.

So Jeannie found them in the morning.

That last day the agony was perpetual. Time after time it lifted her almost off the bed, so they had to fight to hold her down. He could not endure and left the room; wept as if there never would be tears enough.

Jeannie came to comfort him. In her light voice she said: Grandaddy, Grandaddy don't cry. She is not there, she promised me. On the last day, she said she would go back to when she first heard music, a little girl on the road of the village where she was born. She promised me. It is a wedding and they dance, while the flutes so joyous and vibrant tremble in the air. Leave her there, Grandaddy, it is all right. She promised me. Come back, come back and help her poor body to die.

For two of that generation
Seevya and Genya

Death deepens the wonder

The Feminist Press at the City University of New York is a nonprofit literary and educational institution dedicated to publishing work by and about women. Our existence is grounded in the knowledge that women's writing has often been absent or underrepresented on bookstore and library shelves and in educational curricula—and that such absences contribute, in turn, to the exclusion of women from the literary canon, from the historical record, and from the public discourse.

The Feminist Press was founded in 1970. In its early decades, the Feminist Press launched the contemporary rediscovery of "lost" American women writers, and went on to diversify its list by publishing significant works by American women writers of color. More recently, the Press's publishing program has focused on international women writers, who remain far less likely to be translated than male writers, and on nonfiction works that explore issues affecting the lives of women around the world.

Founded in an activist spirit, the Feminist Press is currently undertaking initiatives that will bring its books and educational resources to underserved populations, including community colleges, public high schools and middle schools, literacy and ESL programs, and prison education programs. As we move forward into the twenty-first century, we continue to expand our work to respond to women's silences wherever they are found.

For information about events and for a complete catalog of the Press's 250 books, please refer to our web site: www. feministpress.org.